"DON'T JUDGE ME BY MY SUCCESS IF YOU DON'T KNOW MY STRUGGLES!"

"Another triple platinum gangsta Tale"

WRITTEN BY G PRINCE

SEPTEMBER 19, 2013

www.Ghettotheorywriting@yahoo.com

Copyrights: Ghetto Theory Publishing

ISBN: 978-0-9897486-2-9

<u>*Dedication*</u>

This book is dedicated to all the Hustlers, Player's, Gangsta's, Down Bitches and Gorillas.

Table of Content

Chapter 1
From the Cradle to the Grave

It was the 2nd of July, and Fifty's last day in Clinton Maximum State Prison. Fifty and his four man crew Power, Black, Yayo, and Little Chucky was laying back on the yard sippin on a couple of quarts of that jail house hooch (wine), and watching their little homeboys Crazy legs and Finesse put down a vicious ass woopen on Slim and Ace on the basketball court.

It was like the most anticipated black top game of the year, because these were four of the best ball players to ever fuck off their lives and loose out on their NBA blessings.

Slim and Ace were out of the Forty Projects and both were high school all stars who got caught up on a jewelry store robbery that landed them in prison with a seven year bid.

Crazy Legs on the other hand was considered one of the next Michael Jordan, but came home from a game and caught his step father drunk using his mother like a punching bag and Crazy Legs decided to unload his 3.80 in his step father's face, causing him to receive a six year bid. The murder case was dropped to manslaughter due to the special circumstances that was involved and displayed by the extent of over kill, which showed traces of emotional trauma.

Nevertheless, his NBA dreams went out of the window with the guilty plea, but not his love for the game.

Finesse on the other hand was everything that his name defined. He had the style and grace of Magic, with the finesse of a Globe Trotter, and he could toy with your body on the court as if you where his puppet.

Finesse was a petty drug dealer who knew only one way to eat, and that was by hustling. An NBA contract was the last thang on his mind when he knew that his mother was broke and his brother and sisters was starving because their cabinet was bare. So he knew what he had to do and that was get some money, 'which was his main intentions.'

He messed around and served a cute smoker bitch trying to talk her out of some pussy and come to find out, the bitch was an undercover posing as a smoker, and she was devoted to tricking' hustlers out of their lives.

Finesse cursed himself for thinking with his dick and accepted it as a lesson learned as he pleaded out to a sixteen month bid. However, Clinton was his home now and he was representing with his little homie Crazy Legs as he did a cross over that shook Slim out of his shoe, and then dribbled to the basket as Ace went to try to defend the lay up.

Finesse did a behind the back bounce pass to Crazy Legs that was right on time and Crazy Legs finished with a sweet 360 slam dunk that sent the crowd applauding as they won the game in style.

"Yo Sun, now that was some fly shit." Little Chucky said as he gave Power dap.

"Sun, that nigga's the truth – he'll fuck over any of them NBA niggas, he got mad skills." Yayo said as he gave Fifty dap.

Yo, that nigga was born with wings, I ain't never seen a nigga jump that high." Power said, as he finished off the last of the wine.

"You ain't never lied, but peep Black – go tell that nigga Force to come up off that bread." Fifty said, as he looked over at Black.

Black nodded and went over to where Force and his boys were standing to collect the hundred books of stamps that they bet on the game.

Stamps were considered the currency on the yard. Each book of stamp was worth five dollars per book, and a hundred books is equivalent to five hundred dollars, so basically, Force and Fifty had a five hundred dollars bet on the game.

Black said, "Yo Force, what's up son – need that ends baby! Your boy's tried to pull an up set, but they just didn't make enough baskets!"

Ha, ha, ha," Black laughed at his humor as Force smiled to try to hide his anger.

"Yo Black – I thought that you was just playing Sun, I didn't know that you wanted to bet for real." Force said with a surprised look on his face as his six man crew tried to hold back their grins.

"Wo, Wo, Wo nigga, I know that you're not trying to pull a bluff move on the gorilla himself," Black said.

"Naw man, I wouldn't try to play you, I'm serious! I didn't know that we really had a bet!" Force said with a serious look on his face and tone in his voice.

"Ain't this a bitch – I must be dreaming or something. This can't be real."

Fifty just handed Crazy Legs and Finesse ten books of stamps a piece and looked up and seen tension in his comrade body language, and him and his crew rushed over to Black to see what the problem was. As they approached, he heard his homie say, "This can't be real." And Force and his crew stepped up in battle formation as he seen Fifty and his crew approaching.

"Yo Black, what's the word Sun." Fifty asked.

"Yo Sun, this nigga caught amnesia or something." Black uttered.

"Listen Nigga, I told you that I didn't know that you was serious, what the fuck I'ma bet five hundred dollars on some washed up basketball playing niggas for? I ain't got to beat you niggas out of no crumbs – fool, I got real money!"

Everybody knows that Force is hooked up with Supremes' crew, and all them niggas is known for having big paper. But also, Supremes' crew is out of the Forty Projects and they beef hard with the Guy Brewer projects where Fifty and his crew are out of.

"You're playing with that money gangsta'!" Little Chucky said as Fifty held up his hand to stop Little Chucky's thoughts, before he kick off a war.

"Yo Force, if you said that you didn't make the bet, then we'll take that as your word," Fifty said.

"Man this nigga's lying." Black stated firmly.

"Fool, what the fuck I'ma lie to you fo, you ain't nobody!" Force said in an aggressive manner.

"Hold up nigga, this shit is nothing. All a man got is his word, and if he ain't got no word, then he ain't got no honor or self respect. So, we're going to honor this nigga's word, and let this here small misunderstanding go, feel me?"

Fifty's crew was disappointed at the call, but knew that Fifty just laid down the law and they had to honor it.

"I always knew that you were a smart man." Force said, as he laughed. Ain't you out of here tomorrow?"

"Yeah, and I can't wait to shake this crazy shit!"

"Yeah, check this out – when you get out there, hit your bitch Me'Me' in the ass and once you cum, tell her that it's from me. She loved it when I use to hit that big yellow ass." Force said, as his crew started laughing with him.

"I'll think about it, but first I'ma catch-up with that fine baby's momma that you got, and get some of that bom ass head that she love to give!" Fifty shot back as his crew started bustin' up.

"Yeah, that bitch do got the fire head don't she?" Force said as he grabbed his crotch.

"She sure do!" Yayo uttered out load as everyone started busting up again.

"Fuck you Yayo, we're out of here nigga! Force said, as him and his crew turned and walked away.

"Yo Sun, what the fuck is going on! You guys know that, that muthafucka made that bet – how you gonna' accept that?" Black said as he looked at Fifty for some sort of explanation!

"Who said that we're gonna accept it? Did I say that? Did Yayo say that? What about you Little Chucky did you say that?" Fifty asked with a smile.

"Hell naw, I didn't say that!" Little Chucky said firmly, with a serious look on his face.

"Then what are we going to do about it?" Black asked.

"What do you think that we should do about it?" Fifty asked, as Yayo, Power and Little Chucky all looked at Black for a reply.

"I think that we should smash them!" Black firmly said as Power shook his head in agreement.

"Do ya'll agree too?" Fifty looked at Yayo and Little Chucky.

"You muthafucken right!" Little Chucky said.

"Yo sun, I don't think that I'll be able to sleep at night, if I let that busta get off on me like that!" Yayo said.

"O'kay then, we ride! Gorilla's on the prow!" Fifty said with a smile. "But we got to do this shit right and quick, and after we put this down then we can't let any of his crew back on this yard. You guy's got to hold it down for gorilla only."

"I'm with that!" Black said.

"Me too!" Little Chucky said as he gripped the handle to his 8 inch steal bone crusher knife.

"Well it's law! Now let's go plan this move out. Maybe I can still make my release date."

Yayo looked at his comrade with the utmost respect, because he knew that Fifty was a true gangsta and would be a rider to his dying day. Here he is, hours away from his release date, and willing to risk it all for this respect, integrity, and crew.

"Fifty, we can handle this one, you just stay in the cut and watch our backs so you won't fuck off your date. We need you out there more then in here!" Yayo sincerely uttered as Black and Little Chucky shook their heads in agreement.

"Nigga you must be drunk off that hooch that you just got through drinking, if you think for a minute, that I'ma let that busta get away with disrespecting me and my crew. I'll get out when they let me out – fuck these niggas, we ride!"

"I knew that nigga was going to say that!" Little Chucky said as he laughed and shook his head.

"Me too!" Yayo said. "I just had to say it so he didn't think that we didn't give a damn!" And everyone started laughing as they entered their building. Fifty and his crew was in the same building as Force and his six man crew. So it was really convenient.

Fifty told Little Chucky, Power, and Black to go and get ready and kick back until Yayo come and give them the game on how the move was going down. They agreed and left to go get ready. Fifty didn't want Force and his crew to see him and his crew crowded up like they were plotting and planning something, so he just took Yayo to the room and they put the plan down, and then he had Yayo go and tell Black, Power, and Little Chucky how it was going to go down, and the best time to do it.

Force was in his room with two of his six man crew Big Sam and Zone, as they smoked a joint and talked about how Slim and Ace jacked the game off.

Force said, "I could've made a hundred books, but these niggas ain't got no 'D', Crazy legs and Finesse was fuckin over them Niggas Sun!"

"Yo peep Kid, what if Slim and Ace would've won, and Fifty came at you with that same game?" Zone asked.

"Yo Sun, this muthafucken place would be on lock down right now – I would've gutted that fool on the spot, if he would've came at me with that lame shit. I ain't having it!" Force said, as he hit the joint and past it to Zone.

"Yo Force, what makes you so sure that them niggas is going to except it?" Big Sam asked.

"Man them nigga's some bitches! Fuck them Gorilla crew niggas! That nigga Fifty know how we at the Forty Projects get down, we don't like them fake as Monkeys anyway. And plus, that nigga goes home tomorrow, so I know damn well he ain't going to fuck his date off over no got damn stamps. He ain't that damn crazy." Force uttered in his defense.

"I feel you Sun, but don't sleep on them fools!"

"Man Fuck them niggas, they better be glad that we didn't run all them busta's up out of here. If that nigga Black, say one more slick thing out of his mouth to me, then I'ma smash his bitch ass!" Force said as he lite up a Kool's cigarette and laughed to himself.

* * * *

It was 6:00p.m. and everyone was grabbing their food, wine, Zums and Wams, getting ready to watch the New York Knicks face off with the L.A. Lakers. Fifty was talking to Big Caesar a B.G.F. member who was known for his militant and aggressive behavior, it was known by most, that Big Caesar stabbed over 15 people in his 12 years of incarceration. Five of them was stabbed on the same day. And two of the 15 people was correctional offices. It was said that Big Caesar put on a mask and ran into the lieutenant's office and stabbed the lieutenant and another officer, and then ran out after the officers ran and locked themselves in the bathroom trying to get away from the vicious assault. Once they ran in the bathroom and locked the door, then Big Caesar just walked right out and got away. The officers left their walkie-talkies on their office desk, so when the mask man ran in with a big Jason knife in his hands, the last thing that was on their minds, was a damn walkie-talkie as the lieutenant got hit in the back and shoulder, and the other officer got hit in the face by his cheek and twice in the chest area. They stayed in the bathroom for 10 minutes scared to death waiting for someone to arrive to save them.

"Yo Fifty, I heard about that bogus move that Force pulled on ya'll today. And I don't respect it! If you want, when you leave I'll punish his ass for you!" Big Caesar said, as he looked at Fifty for the approval.

"Hell naw man, your wife is coming up here almost every week and bringing your son and daughter, what kind of friend will I be, if I let you fuck off that blessing on a busta? You know how us Gorilla's get down, we run the jungle Sun. We don't see no sucka's, we eat snakes!"

Big Caesar laughed at his little homie sense of humor, knowing that they both represent the Gorilla, but under a different cause. But a Gorilla embraces and respects another Gorilla always in the jungle of life.

"O'kay Sun, handle yours how you see fit, I know that you're short and sometimes you got to be the bigger man and walk away from stupid shit." Big Caesar stated firmly as he tried to take the sting out of Fifty's humiliation.

"Walk away? Shit I ain't learned how to do that one yet, maybe someday, but not today!" Fifty said, as he laughed and held out his hand to give Big Caesar a hand shake.

Big Caesar smiled and said, "Boy, you're too much like me – I don't know if that's a good thing or bad thing!" And they both laughed!

As Fifty said, "probably both!" And smiled as he walked away.

Fifty entered the T.V. room and seen his crew posted up around, and in back of Forces crew strategically. Force and his crew liked to regulate the T.V., so they always kept chairs in the front row so they could maintain the best view. Fifty went over to Power who was posted in the back and said, "Big Sam is in the shower and Cream is by the microwave cooking. Go and let them know what this Gorilla crews about!" Power just smiled and casually walked away.

Force looked back at Black and said "I like the New York Knicks for 40 books."

Black looked up at the T.V. and seen that the L.A. Lakers was down by 12 points in the middle of the second quarter, and said, "Beat!"

And everyone looked around kind of surprised knowing that Force just bet them out of a hundred books earlier that day.

"Yo ya'll heard that – it's a bet, I don't want no bullshit about my money after this game or it's going to be problems." Force stated as he shook his head.

"Yo Sun, we straight? But, let's shake on it to make it official." Black said with a scandalous grin as Fifty, Yayo, and Little Chucky all know what was coming next.

Force stood up to go shake Black's hand, and once their hands connected, Black pulled Force off balance, and upped his bone crushing big penitentiary knife, and hit Force right in the shoulder blade causing Force legs to collapse.

Yayo jumped up instantly and said, "G-thang fool," and hit Zone right in the jaw with a metal rod that went right through to the other side of his face. Then Yayo snatched it back out and gutted Zone in the lower stomach. Zone cried out in pain as he pushed off of Yayo to get the rod out of his stomach and tripped over a chair trying to get away.

Little Chucky had the back of Rider's shirt and was stabbing Rider in the shoulder, back, and in the back of Riders head as Rider was running dragging Little Chucky trying to get away. Rider finally slid out of his bloody shirt and ran out of the T.V. room.

Fifty socked Zero as Zero tried to run away, and Zero fell down right in front of Little Chucky's feet, as Little Chucky dove on top of him and started stabbing him in the face and chest.

Quon pulled out his knife and squared off with Fifty, but got hit in the head with a lock tide on the end of a belt that Yayo had on him, and knew how to use it. Quan's head busted on impact and he stumbled against the wall, and when he looked up, he felt the cold steal of Fifty's bone crushing blade penetrate his gut. He fell to the ground and curled up as Fifty hit him two more good times and looked up and said "lets roll!"

Little Chucky was in a zone wrestling trying to get a good hit off on Zero as Zero was holding on to Little Chucky's arms for dear life. Yayo kicked Zero in the face to put an end to the wrestling match, and Little Chucky stabbed Zero once again in the face and said, "Got you bitch!"

Yayo pushed Little Chucky off and jumped back as Little Chucky swung his knife wildly off instinct.

"It's me little nigga, let's roll!"

Little Chucky got up and looked over at Force and his face was cut open with a big razor cut. They looked up at Black and Black said, "What can I say, I take pride in my work!"

"Come on let's go!" Fifty said, as they rushed out of the bloody T.V. room.

Once out of the T.V. room they notice Power and Big Caesar walking out of the shower area, and Big Caesar just smiled at Fifty as they all made it to their cells. Fifty and Yayo was cellies and they hurried up and changed their clothes and ran to the laundry room and threw their clothes in a washer that they already had full of water and waiting. A minute later Little Chucky came and threw his and Black's clothes in the same washer machine, and the duces went off, letting the prison guards from everywhere know that a fight or trouble broke out in a certain unit. Fifty, Yayo, and Little Chucky all walked out and seen Quan and Rider carrying Force up to the office, and Big Sam was standing their wet, drenched in blood with his hands covering his stomach wound trying to stop the bleeding. The prison guards ran in yelling, "Lock down, lock down, get in your damn cells, lock down!"

Fifty and Yayo stepped into the cell and Fifty stood in the doorway as the door closed, and was watching as Little Chucky was looking at him smiling, and then he looked up at Big Caesar as Big Caesar hit his chest two times like a Gorilla, and the door closed.

Fifty and Yayo was doing a quick wash up because they knew that it would be a body search. But luckily, nobody got hit or harmed during the move, and Yayo smiled over at Fifty and said, "Now that was a brilliant plan! That's the way the shits suppose to be put down Sun – quick, effective, and easy!"

"Yeah, but it ain't over yet." Fifty said, as he looked out of the cell door window and seen the officers put Quan and Force on the stretchers and carried them away. "Let's just hope that those niggas don't tell or one of these other niggas in here."

"Yo listen Sun, if one of these niggas snitch, then I'll take the case. Fuck it! I got 15 more years any damn way. You just watch over my family and I'll be cool."

"Yo, you know that, that goes without saying any-way." Fifty muttered.

"Yeah I know, if nobody else Sun I believe in you, and when you get out nigga, do me a favor and turn the music industry out."

"You know I am, they better not even let me get my foot in the door, or I'ma change the game because these sucka's ain't rappin about shit! You know that I'm hungry for it, but first I got to get my shit together, because it's hard chasing a dream when you're living fucked up."

"I feel you on that Sun!"

"Body search!" The prison guard yelled as he walked up to Fifty and Yayo cell door.

Yayo walked up with his shirt off and let the guard view his upper body for any scratches, bruises, or holes.

"Next", the prison guard said, as Yayo and Fifty switched places. And the guard started viewing Fifty's upper body for fight marks as the captain of the guards walked up.

"Well, Well, Well, what do we have here? Two of my favorite convicts! I won't even waste my time asking you two about this, but if I find out that you guys is pushing a street beef in my prison, then I'll flood this prison with both of you guys crew, and watch you two kill each other off and I'll let the judge wash up who-ever is left over. So you better hope that I don't find out that this is the issue. Ain't you going home tomorrow?" He looked straight into Fifty's eyes.

"Yeah, and I can't wait to get the hell up out of here.....! I'll probably have nightmares for a long time after leaving here."

"Well I hope that those nightmares will keep your ass out of here, cause too many of you young black men are losing your dreams and substance wasting away behind these walls. And now I got to watch you guys kids come through here and get stabbed, killed, or turned out, just because you males don't want to become a real man. Do yourselves a favor, strive to become a man, and leave all them other ignorant labels alone. And be happy that Force and his crew didn't press charges, because if they did, I'd be reading you your rights, instead of given you this farewell speech. Now get your dumb ass back in the cell. Close cell 7...."

"Damn, that was some deep shit there!" Yayo said.

"I know, I feel like I was holding my breath for the whole five minutes that he was speaking." Fifty said.

"Man, how in the fuck did he find out so quick Sun?"

"I don't know, but I'm glad that Force and his crew didn't jump bitch on us, and press charges!"

"I know, at least now you can leave this muthafucka, we know that much."

"You got-damn-right, and it's my turn to shine Sun! Don't worry, if it's within my power then you'll be out and ballin with me, that's my word!"

"Word is Law-G-thang!" Yayo said as he blast a Newport cigarette up and turned up the radio as Tupac, "All eyes on me," song bumped through the speakers.

Chapter 2
Real Niggas Do Real Thangs

Fifty was up in the morning at 5:45a.m. doing push up's when Yayo woke up and looked up at his comrade flexing in the mirror.

"My bag Sun, didn't mean to wake you!" Fifty uttered as he seen his comrade staring up at him.

"I ain't trippin, I probably wouldn't be able to rest either if I was on my way up out of this hell hole." Yayo stated as he smiled.

"Yo sun, them hoes is going to go crazy over this body...... I can't wait to hit that new Bally's Fitness gym on Jamaica Ave., I'ma clown on them bitches."

"What-cha' gonna' tell-m' Fifty?"

"Go Shorty it's your birthday,- go Shorty it's your birthday, and you can suck it up cause it's your birthday!"

"You're a fool for that one nigga." Yayo said as they laughed.

The prison guard came around and handed out sack lunches and Fifty said, "Yo c/o Smith, do you know what time that I'll be leaving?"

"Yeah, they should come down and get you around seven o'clock. We're on lock down so you got to be escorted to R&D so be ready."

"O'kay cool – appreciate it!"

The C/O walked away and Fifty started gathering all his shit he wanted to leave for his comrades. "Yo, give these new Jordan's to Big Caesar for me, he wears my size and I want to leave him something. And give Power these other two new pair of Jordan's for me too!"

"What are you going to wear out?" Yayo asked looking confused.

"I'ma wear them old Adidas with them old 501's and a T-shirt. I don't need none of that shit – that shit is only fly in here, it's a whole nother world out their."

"I can respect that!"

"Yo now peep, give Little Chucky this watch and my CD player with these 5 CD's and give Black these two Butt man fend books and the blue Tims. You can have the rest of this shit and here, this chain is for you too." Fifty took off his nice fat link chain and gave it to his comrade.

"Good looking out!" Yayo said as he smiled.

"Yo, you got over two hundred books of stamps and two lockers full of food, so you should be straight until I can get on. So watch over the crew and give them the same love that I would give them. And I was thinking, it might be good to start recruiting some more down niggas, because we don't know how this beef is gona' turn out. And maybe it would be good to have more down and thorough...gorillas to strengthen our foundation in here. I believe that a lot of down niggas is gonna' want to be down with us now, because they see how the Gorillas roll."

"I feel you rade, and I'ma see what I can come up with, but not anyone can represent this, so I got to be real selective, you feel me?"

"My thoughts exactly!" Fifty said as he started washing up in the sink and getting himself ready for his resurrection back into the game of life.

* * * *

Fifty arrived at the bus station at 8:30a.m. and he felt like a two ton weight had just been lifted from off his shoulders. He took a deep breath as the fresh air of the musty bus station filled his lungs. He went right over to the little snack shop and brought a cranberry juice, some big red gum, and a big bag of Doritos and a new Vibe magazine. Then he went to the fast food deli and ordered him two double cheese burgers, a thang of french-fries and a thang of onion rings, and then went to go sit on the bus waiting it's departure.

Before the bus left, Fifty saw this cute sista walk on the bus and only three seats was left available to her – his, a fat white man's and an older black lady's, she choose the older black lady seat. Fifty smiled as he thought to himself, "I'll bet a dollar to a bucket of shit, that, that bitch got some drugs in her back-pack," and he gazed down at the black book bag that she sat on the floor of the bus in-between her legs.

Clinton State Prison is located in up state, so it would take about 8 hours before Fifty arrived at the bus station in Queens. Fifty laid back in the seat and relaxed after smashing as much food as he could eat. He was reading an article in the Vibe about Tupac's death, when he seen the young cute sister get up and go into the bathroom in back of the bus and she took her back-pack with her. Fifty knew right then that she was up to no good.

The bus stopped in-between, at another bus station for a ten minute brief pit stop to gas-up, and so the passengers on the bus could stretch and grab some refreshments. Fifty got off and went to buy some more zums and wams, and when he was returning he seen an officer headed toward the bus with a big German Shepard K-9 dog. Fifty went on the bus, and the bus was still kind of empty except for the older black lady who was sitting next to the cute sista. Fifty reached down and grabbed the back-pack and moved it two seats behind where the older black lady was sitting, and placed it under the seat of the fat white man.

The older black lady said, "Sir, what are you doing, that's not yours!"

"I know and I hope that you can keep a secret and trust me, because I will never do anything to hurt you or disrespect you. So please keep this between us!"

The older black lady just looked at him puzzled, but knew better to get involved in matters that don't concern her. The bus filled up quick and the fat white man sat down in his seat and started smashing a pizza that he just brought. The cute sista got on the bus last and was nervous, especially when she seen her bag missing. She asked the older black lady and the older black lady pointed at Fifty and said something. The cute sista looked back at Fifty; and Fifty held up his finger to his lips for her to be quite. And just then the police entered the bus with the German Shepard K-9 dog and the dog was pulling hard trying to get to something.

"Please, we ask that you don't be alarmed we are from DEA and this is just standard procedures. So just stay in your seats and we will be in and out of your way in a minute." The police officer walked the dog down the aisle and the dog ran right for the black backpack that was up underneath the fat white man's seat. The white man looked down in shock, and said, "that's not mine....!"

"Sure it's not, can you please come with us Sir?"

"But that's not mine..... I never saw that bag in my life."

"We know, but can you please come with us Sir!, and I must inform you that you have the right to remain silent, and anything that you say, can and will be used against you in a court of law."

"This is outrageous!"

"And you have the right to an attorney...." the Officer said as they escorted the fat white man off the bus and the bus pulled off.

The older black lady smiled at Fifty and her lips uttered the words, "thank you!"

The cute sista walked back to Fifty seat and asked him, "Do you mind if I sit with you for a while?"

Fifty said, "as long as you're not dirty any more!"

She sat down and said, "How did you know that I was dirty?"

"I guess that you can just consider me a real nigga with a profound perception."

"Is that right? Are you sure that Red didn't send you to spy on me?"

"Who?"

"Red!"

"Naw Shorty, I don't know nobody name 'Red', I know a nigga name 'Blue', but not 'Red'." And Fifty and the cute sista started laughing.

"Where are you from?"

"I'm from Queens!"

"Queens…..! What part?"

"I'm from the Guy Brewer Projects?"

"From the Guy Brewer Projects, and you don't know Red? Some-bodies lying!"

"Listen Shorty, I ain't got no reason to be lying to you, or trying to tickle your ears with game. I don't want nothing from you and you don't owe me a thang. So maybe your disrespectful ass needs to find somewhere else to sit!"

"No, I don't mean it like that!"

"Well how else did you mean it?"

"No I mean, Red is around your projects a lot, and it's hard to believe that you haven't met him."

"Listen baby, I'm fresh out of hells wound, I've been away for 3 years, so it's probably a lot of new faces and names that I'm not familiar with."

"Oh shit, my bad baby – I didn't notice. Damn I should've known by your nice muscular built and that sexy fresh glow that you got about yourself." Fifty blushed at the compliment. "Oh I apologize baby, I thought that Red just hired you to watch my back, but now I know that you must've just peeped my hand. Either

your good or I'm slippin, which ever one, I guess It was to
my benefit this time. Oh damn, I apologize...... My name
is Tonye' but my friends call me Tee-Tee for short."

"Please to meet you, they call me Fifty!"

"Fifty? The Fifty from the Gorilla crew?"

"Have we met before?"

"No we haven't met, but I heard a lot of thangs about
you!"

"I hope that you're not the type of person who
believes everything she hears!"

"No but it's nothing wrong with a sista holding on to
the juicy stuff, if you know what I mean!"

"No I don't." Fifty said with a blushful smile.

"Listen Tee-Tee, I'm fresh out and I'm not trying to let
the world know right now, because I probably got more
enemies and haters then friends, so if you can do me a
favor and keep my name off your lips for a minute, then
I'll be grateful. A nigga don't want to get shot before he
can get him a gun, if you know what I mean?"

"Don't worry baby, I'll keep your secret, I promise!
And if you ever need a friend then you can find me at the
strip club called the Attic, it's on Rockaway Blvd."

"Yo ma, if your man is this baller ass nigga name Red,
then why do he have you working at a strip club?"

"First of all, Red is not my man, he's just a business
associate that I make extra money with from time to time,
nothing more and nothing less. And I strip because I like
to dance and the money is real good too. You should try it
yourself, you'll probably be rich with a body like yours,
and I heard that you pack a nice package too!" Tee-Tee
added with a seductive giggle.

"Yeah right-me a stripper, shit I got to be on all kinds
of drugs to do that!" And they both started busting-up. "I
ain't got a problem with slangin some pipe to make the
ends meet, but to get up butt ass naked on a stage in some
tiger stripe swim trunks, I got to pass on that!"

Tee-Tee was crackin-up with tears rolling down her cheeks, "Boy your crazy!"

"Not crazy enough to do that!" And they both laughed together. "Naw but trip, on the serious side you better hope that, that nigga Red believes your story, or he's gonna' put a foot in that pretty ass of yours."

"Shit he better believe me, because I'm not going for that ass woopen shit, he can save that crazy stuff for his Hoochies." Tee-Tee said, in her best woman like voice.

"Yeah, so what are you going to do if he kicks your ass?" Fifty asked to test her thoroughness.

"I don't know, but it won't be nothin' nice!"

Fifty gave her credit for not being stupid enough to say something to get herself caught in a trick bag.

The bus pulled up to the bus station in Queens and Tee-Tee looked at Fifty and said, "I had a real nice time kicking it with you and I'm grateful for the way you had my back, thank you!" Then she lend over and gave Fifty a kiss on the cheek.

Fifty smiled and said, "Shorty, I'm a real nigga, that's what we do!" Then he got up and walked off the bus without looking back. He thought in his mind, 'checkmate!'

As soon as Fifty walked out of the bus station in Queens he knew that he was at home. People were hustling everywhere trying to make a buck, and game was played at a all time high. Fifty seen Tee-Tee go and get into a Red Corvette, and the car didn't move for a minute. It looked like they was arguing about something, and then police cars and police came from every-which direction and surrounded the Red Corvette with guns drawn.

"Damn that's wild." Fifty uttered as he said, 'taxi....!' And went to jump in the back of the taxi and watched Tee-Tee and a light skin dude with long hair get pulled out of his Vett by the police and started searching them. Tee-Tee looked up and seen Fifty pass by in the taxi, and just gave

25

a quick smile as she laid hand cuffed across the front of the police car. Fifty said to himself, 'now I know that you owe me big time for that one', he smiled as he said, "take me to the Guy Brewer Project in Rochdale Village" to the cab driver.

Chapter 3
Let the Games Begin

The taxi pulled up at the Guy Brewer Projects and
Fifty knew that he was at home now, he saw niggas posted
up slangin drugs, crack heads running around looking like
Zombies, and young and old ladies running around
dressed sexy trying to show off their best attributes. It was
dejavu as he looked up and saw his comrade Juice serving
a smoker. Fifty stepped out of the taxi and all eyes were
on him. Juice said, "I'll be damn! Look what just jumped
out of the banana mobile!" Fifty smiled as they walked up
to one another and gave each other their secret hand shake
and a gangsta embrace.

"What's up Sun?"

"What's up Juice!"

"Look at you looking all swoll and shit! I heard that
you was putting in work up state!"

"Of course Sun, you know how we do it, and me and
the family appreciate the love that you shown us."

"Ah Sun, you know that I had to look out for my
comrades. When did you get out?"

"Today, I just touched down."

"Oh shit, I know that you want to get your nuts out of
the sand Sun, and I know just the right bitch too…. Tina!
Sun, that bitch can suck a bowling ball throw a water hose,
I'm telling you – that bitch is the truth!"

"Naw, I'm cool right now – I'll take a rain check!"

"OH, what you want some pussy instead? I got a bad
young bitch name Fay that would fuck your brains out for
a C-Note, don't worry I got you – the bitch is a stripper
and she can crush a strawberry with her pussy and make it
spit out the stem."

"Fo real?"

"Yo Sun, I wouldn't shit you!"

"Yo I'm gonna definitely take a rain check on that one! But check it out, I'm financially embarrassed right now... I ain't got a pot to piss in or a window to throw it out of. And I'm naked out here!" Fifty said; with a serious expression on his face.

"Yo Sun don't worry, I got you! Hey Tank!"

"What's up Juice?"

"Where is Ra' and Little G-nut at?"

"They're in big Michelle's apartment!"

"Yo, tell them that I said to come and holla at me right now!"

"Yo, I'm on it!"

"Ra', Little G-nut? I don't remember them." Fifty said curiously.

"Of course not Sun, these are our little comrades – I recruited them myself and they are as thorough and gangsta as it gets. You know that the older homies had a big shoot with the Supreme crew a while back, and when the police arrived the homies turned their guns on the pigs and it was ugly. Five homies got killed in that shoot out and three police. Big Game, R.J. and Earth all hit death row behind it, and Tec, P-Funk and Ghost is on the run, they ran to different states. Now it's me, G-5, and Seven and the six little homies that we recruited. I put down Ra, Baby Tank, and Little G-nut. And G-5 put down Baby Game, and G-Pain, and Seven put down Little Ghost. But them niggas Fakin, they're doing their own thang! Me and my little rades is the ones holding it down."

"Why didn't you get word to me about this incident with our comrades and the police?" Fifty said in a angry voice!

"I did, I told Me-Me and gave her the news paper clippings and the obituaries. She said that she sent it to you along with the $300 dollars that me and the little homies sent to ya'll."

"What $300 dollars? All we got was the $500 dollars that you gave my grandmother to send me twice."

"Yo sun, you're bullshitting! Me and the little homies been sending you guys $300 dollars up there every other month, and sometimes more when that bitch Me-Me tell us that your broke."

"Man that bitch ain't sent me a crumb since I been down – that's my word Sun!"

"Man bitch is in violation Sun, she's been playing us like monkeys Fifty! How do you want to proceed with this Sun? I could send my little crew over there and they'll do something big with her Sun. Just give me the word!"

"Naw, Naw! That ain't the way to go! I got this J, just keep the intricacies a secret. I'll deal with the betrayal." Fifty said, as his eyes tightened.

"Cool! Yo, there they go!" And Juice, young Silver Backs walked up looking cautious and confused.

"Yo, what's up Juice?" Ra' said.

"Yo, what's up young nigga's I want you guys to meet someone. This is the nigga who put me on and gave me my name, this is our comrade Fifty. He laid the concrete to this crew, and I'm sure that ya'll heard of him."

"Yo, what's up Sun, we've been waiting for you!" Ra said as he gave Fifty the secret hand shakes.

"Fifty this is Ra, that's Little G-nut, and this Baby Tank."

Fifty gave all of them secret handshake as he looked them over. They had to be between 17 to 19 years old, but looked like they was wise beyond their years. Ra' was the tallest, standing 6'2" with a medium built, dark brown complexion and sportin a short fade, waved up to perfection. Baby Tank on the other hand was a short 5'8" country built brother, who was a dark brown complexion, and wore his hair with French- braids in a fancy design. Little G-nut was considered the pretty boy, he looked like he was black mix with Puerto Rican, he stood 5'10" with a slim built, light gold complexion and long wavy hair that he wore in a pony tail.

"What's up Fifty – it's a honor to meet you man!" Little G-nut said.

"Yeah Sun, you're a legend in these streets." Baby Tank said.

"Yo, I appreciate the sentiments Rades, and thank you for sending me and the family the money that you often sent, you represent honor, respect, and loyalty to this family, and we honor your presence!"

""That's real Sun, that's how we get down." Little G-nut stated.

"Yo Rades," Juice called out, "Your comrade just touched down and he's naked and broke! What are we going to do about that?"

"Yo Sun, I got a brand new 45 automatic for you Rade, straight out the box. I got it from a smoker last night. Here! I did't even get a chance to bust on a nigga yet." Little G-nut said as he handed Fifty the big black 45 automatic and smiled.

"Hold up, we need to have a young gorilla meeting real quick." Ra' said as he called Little G-nut and Baby Tank to the side.

"Fifty laughed and looked at Juice! Juice said, "Shit, your guess is as good as mine!"

"O'kay Rade listen, we ain't ballin!"

"Not by a long shot!" Little G-nut interrupted Ra'.

"But we can spare a little something to keep your pockets from bleeding – here!"

Then Ra' handed Fifty $1,500 dollars and said, "I know that it ain't much, but it's a start!"

"Yo, I appreciate the love, believe me it's enough to get me started." Fifty said with a respectful smile.

"Yo Sun, I got a old school 77 Cutless right ther you can have. It's in cherry condition and it's very low key." Juice said as he gave Fifty the keys.

"It's registered to my girl's auntee, Wendy Jones. All of the tags and paperwork is straight, so you should not get pulled over for nothing. Here's the pink slip," and Juice reached into his wallet and pulled out the pink slip and gave it to Fifty. "Here's fifteen more hundred to make sure that your needs is met.

"Yo Rade, much love Sun. You know once I get on, then I'ma make sure that we all eat good!"

"I hope so," Baby Tank said, "Because we're light weight starving out here."

"Is that right, ain't you guys hustling?"

"Yeah, but these prices is too damn high. And that nigga Red ain't playing fair. If you want to buy an ounce from him, he's going to charge you $700 dollars an ounce, and he's giving it to his workers for $600 dollars an ounce, so they can undercut us. And them Jamaicans won't fuck with us, because the O G homie beat one out of some work a while back, and the Puerto Ricans is only sellin' birds, so if your not pushing weight, then you got to fuck with Red, and he's jewin' the shit out of us, because his shit ain't that good – he steps on it too much."

"Don't worry Rade, things is about to change – believe that! Fifty uttered with a promising grin.

"Yo, let's hook him up with Tina! I know you're trying to empty your clip!" Ra' said.

"Not right now player, I got a lot of catching up to do, maybe next time!"

"Okay, I feel you! Ra' said.

"Yo Juice – Rade I got to run and go see my spiritual soulmate. Let me catch back up with you soon!"

"I feel you Rade, give G-mom my love Sun!"

"Yo Sun, come back soon! Here this is our cell phone numbers and big Michelle's apartment number if you need us for anything, then just call." Little G-nut said as he handed Fifty the paper.

"Yo, let me write mine down too Rade!" Juice said as he took the paper and put his house and cell phone number down.

"Yo, we need to throw a get together for you – you know, a all you can eat, all you can fuck bar-b-que!" Baby Tank said as everyone started laughing.

"When the time is right, then we'll do it big, but for now, let's paper chase!" Fifty said.

"I'm with you on that Rade!" Ra' said.

"Me too Sun!" Little G-Nut' agreed.

Fifty gave his comrades their secret hand shake and jumped in the old school Cutless and rolled out. He went to go get a motel room over at the Q Motor Inn, off of Jamaica Ave., then went to the Green Acres Mall to grab some decent cloths. The mall was packed, it was July 3rd. and everyone seemed to be out buying something new and fly to wear. Fifty looked down at his old penitentiary tennis shoes and said, "We been through a lot together, but it's time for us to part," and smiled as he slid on the brand new fresh Jordan's. Fifty ran store to store grabbing the baddest clothes that was within his budget, even though he had to sensor his taste until a better day.

An hour and a half later, Fifty was in his car counting his money. "Damn, I spent $1600 dollars already." He thought to himself. I got to make a move quick, or I'ma be fucked up soon. Fifty shook his head and drove back to his Motel room so he could wash that 3 year old worth of prison smell off of him, and throw on something worth wearing.

After a nice hot shower, some cologne and a shot of Hennessy, Fifty felt like a new man as he gazed into the mirror at his profile, as he sported some fresh designer jeans, a nice Fubu sweater, and some new suede Tims. "Now that's what I'm talking about!" Fifty uttered as he grabbed his keys and walked out of the motel room door feeling like a million dollars.

As Fifty stepped out of his motel room he spotted this cute Red bone sista' that was thick in all the right places and by the way she was dressed, it was obvious to any player that she was a seasoned hoe. She smiled at Fifty as they passed by one another, and Fifty just gave her a player grin and keep walking by. The cute red bone sista' looked back to see if Fifty was stirring at her big ass like everyone else did, and when she notice that he didn't even look back, she said to herself, "he must be gay.... what a waste," and kept walking and switching her way on to the sidewalk down Jamaica Ave.

Fifty saw the prostitute reflection off his driver side window as she looked back at him, and he just smiled to himself.

"Maybe I should try pimpin' – hoe money is slow money, but fo-sho money!"

Fifty laughed to himself then jumped in his car and drove off.

Fifty pulled up in front of a house that he was all too familiar with, his grandmother's house. She was the one who raised him and made sure that he knew what true love was really about.

Fifty considered her his guardian angel and eternal soulmate. Fifty knocked on the door and the curtains moved to the side and his angel face appeared as her eyes lit up and she quickly opened up the door and said, "My baby, my baby's home! Look Pa it's my baby!"

Fifty's grandmother ran into his arms, as his big powerful frame engulfed her into his warm embrace.

"I told you that I'll be home soon!" Fifty emotionally uttered into her ear as they embraced.

"What you do, break out? Fifty's grandpa said with conviction.

"Naw Pa, I did my time – my debt is paid in full to society."

"Well, they should've kept your ass, because you probably will be back soon; anyway!"

"Pa, that ain't no way to be speaking to your grandson!"

"Hell ma, it's the truth! That boy don't want to do good! Look at him, he's probably plottin' to commit a crime, or plottin' to do something crazy as we speak!"

"Naw Pa, it ain't like that no more! I'm trying to pursue a music career and do something legit for a change!" Fifty said in his defense, but knew that his grandfather didn't cut no corners or bite his tongue, so it won't be an easy task to convince him.

"See Pa, people can change and our baby wants to do something positive. He want's to be an artist!" Fifty grandma said as she looked up at Fifty with proud eyes.

"Artist my ass! That boy can't sing a lick, how in the hell is he going to be and artist!"

"Pa, I don't mean sing – I mean rap...... I want to be a rapper!" Fifty said proudly.

"See Pa, he's going to be a rapper!"

"You mean like grandmaster Flash and the Furious Five, and Run D.M.C.?"

"Yeah Pa, I didn't know that you listen to that!" Fifty said.

"I was young too once you know, I wasn't always this damn old!" They all started laughing! "If you can rap, then let me here you then?" Fifty's grandpa said.

"Yeah let us hear you?" Fifty's grandmother said with excitement in her voice.

"O'kay I wrote this one for you grandma, listen to this!"

Fifty started reciting a rap that he wrote for his grandmother displaying the love that he had for her, and thanking her for loving him. And after he finished his grandmother had tears in her eyes and said, "I love it, it was beautiful! See Pa.... our baby's going to be a rap star!"

"Yeap, he's pretty good! And to think; I thought that you just had dreams of being a criminal!"

"Pa! be nice to the boy."

"Well I did!"

"Naw grandpa, sometimes a man got to do what a man got to do to survive in these streets. I'm not proud of having to struggle through the pains of life in order to reach my success, but if that's what I got to do, then that's what I'ma do, because sometimes we have no choice, it's either swim or die! Fifty sincerely uttered.

"Well, I'm glad that I taught your ass how to swim, because I see too many of them weak minded men drowning in this pool of life. They either die young, get messed off on drugs, or lose their life forever in them prison walls. I can't tell you how many times your grandma cried herself to sleep worrying about you in prison."

"Pa......!"

"No Ma, he got to hear it! Now you got talent, a gift, and a plan, now you need to do what you have to do to make it! Pursue your goals and conquer your dreams and just like Ma cried thinking about your down falls, I want you to make her smile upon your success, and make us proud of you. If not, then kill yourself and save us the stress!"

"Pa..!"

"Ma, I'm just keeping it real! This nigga is gonna' make me turn into a damn alcoholic!" Then everyone started busting-up.

"I hear you Pa- I'll either get rich or die trying!" Fifty said as he smiled at his grandpa. Grandma just shook her head as she held her head down low and whispered "Lord help us!

It was 10:30 p.m. when Fifty left his grandma's house, and he was stuffed from eating the fat steak, eggs, and grits that his grandmother cooked for him.

He was in a good mood when he left, and drove around the New York City streets for a couple of hours, and took in all the beautiful lights and buildings that complimented his new life of freedom.

Fifty pulled up into his motel parking lot at 12:20a.m., and decided to walk to the liquor store before it closed, he grab some cranberry juice to go with his pint of Hennessy and a six pack of Miller Genuine Draft beer to satisfied his long awaited urge. While he was their he grabbed some zums and wams and a six pack of Magnums to satisfy his other urge.

On the way back, Fifty saw a nice new blue Cadillac Seville parked on the side of the curb and he saw two people tussling inside. He casually gazed out-of the corner of his eye as he past, he noticed that it was the same cute thick red bone hooker fighting with this older white man.

Fifty said, "What the hell," and walked over to the driver's side door and knocked on the window with his new big black 45 automatic.

The white man saw the big ass gun, and his eyes got big as Fifty said, "Roll down the damn window before I bust it!"

The white man nervously rolled down the window....

Fifty said, "What the fuck are you doing hitting my bitch like that?"

The hooker smiled and the white man said, "I wasn't trying to hurt her!"

"What's his damn problem?" Fifty asked the hooker.

"This muthafuckas mad that he came to fast when I was giving him head, and now he don't wanna' pay me."

"Is that right? Yo, empty your damn pockets fool." Fifty said, as he pointed the gun at the white man and the white man pulled out a fat wad of bills and Fifty said, "Now give her the whole damn stack before I kick your ass!" The white man hurried up and handed the hooker the wad of bills. "Now give me your damn wallet chump!" The white man reached in his back pocket and gave Fifty the wallet.

"Here take it, just please don't hurt me!"

"You're the one around here trying to hurt people, if it was good like that – then why didn't your dumb ass just pay for seconds? Now it's going to cost you way more."

Fifty looked in the wallet and seen a fat wad of hundreds and fifty dollar bills, and pulled them out and slid them in his pocket.

"Let me see who you are!"

Then Fifty looked through the wallet and saw a unlimited Platinum Visa and a unlimited Platinum Chase Master Card. "Oh you're ballin, who we got here? Oh shit, Doctor Lewis Welch heart surgeon! What a pleasant surprise.

Now listen here dumb dumb! I'ma hold on to these unlimited credit cards and take my girl here shopping for the abuse that you put on her, now if you try to call the police or report these cards stolen, then I'ma let them people know that your around here molesting and raping minors. Because she's only 17 years old, fool!

Now picture the headlines, and now picture your whole career gone!

Also, I know where you work and live at, so do something stupid if you want too! After I get through going shopping I'll call you at this number, 'and he held up the doctors business card', and I'll tell you when to report your cards stolen, don't worry they're insured! And after that, I'll put your wallet in the mail box so you can get your ID's back. Do I make myself clear?"

"Yes.....!"

"Where is the rubber that he was wearing?" Fifty asked the hooker.

"He got it on!"

"Well take it off him!" She reached over and pulled the rubber off his dick.

"Since you're a doctor I know that you know about DNA evidence, so try me and well see who evidence is the best!"

"I won't do nothing stupid, please don't call the police and report me. Take the money and credit cards, just don't report this please." The white man bagged!

"It looks like we got some understanding! Now sweetie, do you want to get your lick back?" The hooker looked at Fifty, then at the white man, and when the white man turned to look at her, she socked him right in the jaw, causing him to grab his cheek and looked at Fifty.

"Now let this be a lesson to you Doc., don't put your hands on women – do you understand?" The white man shook his head yes!

"Come on bitch let's go!" Fifty uttered as the hooker smiled and got out of the car and started walking along side Fifty.

The hooker said, "So I guess that I owe you one," as they walked down Jamaica Ave.

"Nope! Just give me my cut from the wad that he gave you and we're straight."

She looked at Fifty and pulled out the wad from her boot leg and started counting it. It was $900 dollars, she gave Fifty $500 dollars and she kept the rest for herself.

"Good looking out! Nice doing business with you – take care!" Fifty said as he started walking away.

"Wait, wait, what are you doing tonight?"

"I'm just relaxing, bout to kick back and watch a movie!" Fifty said in a nonchalant way.

"Do you want some company?"

"Naw I'm cool, don't you got some money to make – your man is gonna' kick your ass if you ain't got that paper right."

"I don't have no man – I work for myself!" The hooker said proudly.

"Well Shorty, you're barking up the wrong tree because trickin's against my religion!"

"Who said anything about money? I just asked if you wanted some company." She looked at him seductively as they reached his motel room door and she said, "I give good back rubs!"

"I bet you do and good head too according to your most recent consumer!" Fifty said and smiled.

She giggled and said, "Everything I got is the bomb!"

"Damn Shorty! I wouldn't be a boss player if I accepted. You know the game bitch, it's a chosen fee to bathe with a real player. So get your money right and choose, loose, or stay confused." Fifty smiled when he seen the shock look on her face and stepped into his room and closed the door in the cute thick red bone sista face.

"No this black ass nigga didn't just dis the shit out of me like that! Ain't no nigga ever turned down this pussy like that." The hooker turned and walked away toward her motel room in a daze, sprung on the way that Fifty made her feel.

Fifty closed the motel room door and smiled to himself at the way he counteracted the bitches' moves.

He knew that the bitch was trying to play her way into a cut of the credit cards profit, and thought if she gave him some pussy for free, then he'll take her shoppin with him in the morning.

He grabbed his dick and said, "Money over bitches, you know the rules" and started laughing, as he counted the money that he took off of the doctor.

It was $4,400 hundred dollars plus the $500 hundred that he got from the hoe, brung his profit to $4,900 dollars, not including the $1200 hundred that he had left over from what his homies gave him, which brings his bank roll to $6,100 dollars.

"Damn what a difference a lick makes. Fifty thought to himself as he started looking through the wallet.

"Bingo!" He said as he held up the doctor's medical I.D. card with no picture on it.

"It's on now, " Fifty said as he poured himself a shot of Hennessy and cut on the radio as Biggie Smalls song 'Juicy' was bumping through the speaker.

Chapter 4
Paper Chasing

It was the 4th of July and Fifty was up at 6:45a.m.
doing his normal routine of 10 sets of 50 push ups, and 10
sets of 40 sit ups. It was 7:10 when he finished, so he
jumped in the shower then got dressed in a white Polo
dress shirt, and some nice black slacks with some suede
Balley's dress shoes to complete his professional
appearance.

He grabbed his needed necessities and was out the
door by 8:45. He went and enjoy a delicious breakfast at
the pancake house, and after eating, he went over his plan
and headed straight over to the check cashing place off
Linden Blvd., and walked in with an air of confidence in
his stroll.

He was nervous, but he knew that all they could do
is reject his request to withdraw money off his credit cards.
As he walked up to the window, a young lady looked up
at him that he knew from his old high school days. They
went to August Martin High together, she looked at him
and smiled because she was surprised to see him.

He said, "excuse me Maam', I would like to withdraw
a cash advancement off of my credit card," and he place
the platinum Visa in the tray slot.

"Oh, Doctor Lewis Welch," the young lady said with a
small giggle.

Do you have any I.D. sir?" She asked, as Fifty placed
the doctor's certified medical I.D. card in the tray slot.

"O'kay, One minute please!" The young casher said
as she walked over to the back and gave the information to
the fat brown skin sista who was sitting at the back desk.
They whispered for a minute, and then the young casher
came back and asked, "Sir, how much would you like to
withdraw?"

"The max would be fine!" Fifty said with a smile.

"That would be $5,000 dollars sir, but a part from the 5% percent service charge that the check cashing union charges for its service fee, there will also be an additional 10% percent service charge for the insurance policy!" The young casher said with a smile.

"Of course, I wouldn't think less!"

Fifty knew that his friend from school and the lady in the back was charging him an extra $500 dollars for them doing a withdrawal for him without proper I.D. The casher counted out $4,250 dollars and gave it to him. Fifty said, "Thank you Ms., and while I'm here, I might as well take the cash advancement off this one to, because I got a lot of things to do." And he slid the casher the unlimited Platinum Master Card.

"One minute Sir", the casher said as she went to the back and talked to the fat lady then came back and said, "Master Card carries a 20% percent insurance policy rate instead of the 10% percent that Visa carries, is that acceptable to you?" She asked with a conning smile.

"No problem Maam!" Fifty said, with a how-can-I argue grin on his face.

The young casher gave Fifty $3,750 dollars and said, "Have a pleasant day sir, and please come again!"

"I sure will." Fifty said as he walked out of the check cashing place $8,000 thousand dollars richer. He jumped in his car and smiled as he headed to the Green Acres Mall with two fresh unlimited platinum credit cards.

Fifty walked right into the most popular jewelry store, and knew that he had to play his hand to the Tee! He seen an old Jewish lady behind the counter and thought to himself, the perfect 'Vic'.

"Hello Maam, how are you doing today?"

"Fine Sir and you?"

"Well for the most part, I have to admit today is a wonderful day."

"Oh, that's nice......! How may I help you sir?"

Well Maam, I'm a Doctor – a heart surgeon, and my company just closed a big multimillion dollar deal with Global Medical Insurance Corporation, who's like the largest medical insurance corporation in the world. You got to excuse me, but I'm so excited!"

"That's o'kay, you should be!" The old lady said basking in Fifty's excitement.

"Thank you! Well anyway, I was trying to think of a special gift to give my associates and employees, and my wife mentioned that jewelry would be a real nice gift to give. So here I am."

"Well your wife is absolutely right, there's no better gift then a nice piece of jewelry."

Well lets begin with my board of directors. Do you have any nice watches?"

"Yes, over here Sir."

"Oh yeah, Rolex is timeless! O'kay let me have that Povade Presidential Edition for Rob, and that platinum burgundy one and also that black face platinum one. Yes, Steve and Joe will like that! And let me have that man's diamond bracelet, yes that's nice, you wouldn't have the chain to go with it would you? Oh yeah, a perfect match. O'kay let me have that four caret princess cut diamond ring, and that one there too! And I need a woman's diamond bracelet, yes let me have both of them, and both of them diamond ankle bracelets too. Yes Jan would like that, because she has lovely legs. You better give me that three and half carat diamond Rolex ladies ring too, that one too, because my wife would never forgive me if I forget her. And yes one more thing let me have those single carat diamond ear rings. My secretary would hate me if I forgot her. Wow, that should do it! How much do I owe you?"

"Sixty-six thousand dollars Sir!" The old Jewish lady said with a hungry smile.

Fifty reached into his wallet and pulled out the platinum visa card. Then the old lady said, "One minute Sir." And went to make a phone call, and then came back and gave Fifty a receipt to sign and after Fifty scribbled his new alias name down, the old lady said, "Thank you so much Doctor Welch, and please come again Sir!"

"I sure will Maam, have a nice day!"

"You too Sir!"

Fifty laughed with excitement as he went back to his car and stashed the jewelry in the trunk. Then went back in the Mall and went to the most popular urban clothes store in the mall. A middle age Italian man walked up to Fifty and said, "What's up player – whatcha looking for? I got the new Sean John, Roc-a-wear, Guess, Phat Farm, Nautica, Fubu, causal wear, suits, Gator foot wear – whatever you want baby I got you!"

Fifty knew that he had a hyped hustler here, so he had to use the right approach. Fifty said, "Well, my company just received a big multimillion dollar contract with a very big Global Medical Insurance Corporation, and my wife keeps telling me that I need to up grade my wardrobe, see I'm a doctor, and I guest that I'm use to dressing down because I work so much."

The Italian man looked at Fifty and said, "listen player, I don't give a damn if you're a freakin' Astronaut today, if that credit card slides through that machine over there, then you can have anything in this store that you want – *CAPISH*....!"

"O'kay, well I'll take a little bit of everything." Fifty said with a grin.

"You got it player – check these new Sean John sweat suits out, we just got them in yesterday!"

Fifty found his mark and went on a buying frenzy. He brought everything that caught his eye, everything from jeans, sweat suits, sweaters, and coats.

He even brought a black quarter length mink jacket and eight silk Versace suits.

Then he made sure that his shoe game was on point, with five pairs of gators and five pairs of Eel skin boots to compliment his suits and slacks.

He brought ever color and style Tims and Jordans'. He even brought eight Sean John female sweat suits, five Gucci dresses; three pairs of Gucci boots, a nice $1000 dollar Gucci purse, seven nice female Roc-a-wear Jeans, and five Roc-a-wear sweaters and Sean John female leather jacket.

After he got through; his credit card bill was $43,000 dollars and the Visa worked like a charm.

Fifty went and put all of the clothes in the trunk of his car and went back in to Robinson May and went at it again.

He grabbed 10 packs of boxer underwear, 10 packs of T-shirts, 10 packs of wife beaters, and 10 packs of socks with 20 different pairs of silk socks.

Then he grabbed all of the fly colognes and three nice Victoria Secret perfume sets, then stop by the woman's department and grabbed ten sundresses and six Teddy's lingerie sets.

Fifty knew that the game was about to change, and he was about to make sure that he was in control.

He pulled up to an elegant town house apartment on the South Side in a nice and quiet neighborhood and saw a 'For Rent' sign in the yard. It read 2 bedroom and 1 1/2 bathroom newly remodeled Town House for $1,400 per month.

Fifty got out of his car and went to the manager's apartment and knocked on the door. An older light skin sista answered holding a big baby in her arms and said, "May I help you?"

"Yes Maam, I was interested in the apartment that you have for rent."

"Oh yes, it's a nice two bedroom that's been remodeled and the asking price is $1,400 a month."

"Well do you mind if I could see it?"

"Sure, let me grab the keys…!" James, come and get your little brother for me, so I could go show someone the apartment next door."

"Mom, I'm playing with my Sega Genesis!"

"Boy, if you don't get your butt down here and do what I said, then I'ma get rid of that damn game!"

The little boy hurried up and came down the stairs to get his 18 month old baby brother. The boy little James had to be around 7 years old, he grabbed his brother and mean mugged Fifty as he went back up stairs.

"These kids and those damn games, I barely can get him to go outside now!" The woman said as she escorted Fifty to the third town house with two more on the same lot – five units total. She opened up the door and started showing Fifty around, it was a two story set up with both the bedrooms up stairs and living room, dining room, and kitchen down stairs. Fifty knew that it was perfect for him, but now wondered if he could finesses his way into it.

"How do you like it?"

"It's nice, how much to get in?"

"Well, its first, last and security which would come up to $3,000 dollars for the move in cost."

"That sounds reasonable, but I'm currently relocating here and I haven't found stable employment yet. But I do have the money to move in and I'll also be willing to pay a two month in advance to cover the next two months rent. That should hold me until I find a good job."

"I don't know Sir!"

"How bout I give you $500 hundred dollars extra for your trouble and assistance."

"Let me get this straight, you're gonna' give me first, last, security, and two months rent paid in advance, plus

$500 hundred dollars for me letting you have it right now?"

"Yes!"

"Who name do you want it in?"

"You can use mine- I don't owe no debts or anything."

"Well come and fill out the application and if they approve you, then I will too, but please keep this between us. I'll lose my manager job and have to move, if this gets out!"

"Trust me!" Fifty said with a smile as the lady said, Come on then." And they went to her apartment to fill out the paperwork. Fifty had an old fake I.D. that he barely used before he got busted, and he retrieved it from his grandmother's house when he was over there, it was the name that he used to put the apartment in, because he didn't want no unwanted visitors early in the morning, especially if the police ever decide to look for him, for any reason. This way he can have a place to rest that no one would know about.

Fifty walked out of the town house complex with keys in hand. It was only 3:30p.m. so he knew that he had enough time to put his second lick down. Fifty pulled into the U-haul truck rental company and rented a big moving truck. They charged him an extra $500 dollars for security, because he had to use his real driver license to rent the truck and not the fake credit cards. Nevertheless, Fifty was on a roll as he pulled up to an exotic furniture store.

"Greetings my friend, how may I be of service to you!" the Indonesian man asked.

"Yes, I just purchased a new home on Madian Ave., and I was looking for some Contemporary Furniture to decorate it with.

"Well sir, you come to the right place, we have the finest assortment of soft leather couches and chairs that money can buy."

"I see, Fifty said as he sat on a soft leather egg shell white chair that included a love set, sofa, and two chairs set up, how much for this set?"

"Yes that's a nice one; that goes for $6,000 dollars for the set."

Fifty asked, "And what about that dark burgundy marble table set?"

"This set is 100% real marble hand crafted with an exotic swirl pattern to compliment the style, and also that marble audio and entertainment cabinet is included for the sell price of $4,000 dollars."

"Do you have a dining room set that will compliment this set up?"

"Of course sir, this is a beautiful hand crafted marble table that sits eight people and it comes with these marble decorated chairs with the off white leather cushions."

"Perfect!"

"The dining room set is $4,500 dollars, but we're having a sale on this piece today for $3,000 out the door!"

"O'kay, I also need a couple of bedroom sets."

"Yes, come with me sir. Over here is where you would find the bedroom sets to remember."

"Say no more, I'll take that burgundy one and the black one."

These are hand crafted red wood with a lacquer base, with a sophisticated top frame that holds up the nylon see through curtains. Both beds sets cost you $4,000 dollars a piece including the two dressers. Will you need the mattresses and box spring as well?"

"Yes, the King size along with the pillows and sheets!"

"Here, as Fifty handed the store owner his Platinum Master Card along with the Doctor's I.D. card. Fifty was hoping that he won't ask for more identification.

"Oh Doctor Welch, It's a pleasure to meet you. My brothers a doctor too, he's a neurosurgeon top of his class, his name is Doctor Issisy. Do you know him?"

"As a matter of fact, I think that I met a doctor by that name before, at a medical convention I believe."

"Yes, he attends there often too!"

"Yes, I can't really remember him but I believe that I heard that name before."

"Yes, he's an excellent surgeon - one of the best!"

"It's a blessing - do you think that you can have your workers load this stuff on my truck for me – I got my nephews meeting me over to the new house to help me unload it."

"Oh you brung your own truck, good, good, I'll give you a discount since we don't have to deliver it."

"Beautiful….!"

"I'll be right back with your receipt!"

"Great."

The store owner came back and handed Fifty the receipt with the credit card and fake medical I.D., and Fifty signed the receipt and gave the loader's the keys to the big U-haul truck, and they started loading up the truck to capacity!"

Fifty pulled off 25 minutes later with a big smile on his face, and now he had to find some reliable help that he could trust to help him unload the truck. He drove by a park 10 blocks from his town house and seen two young teenage boys playing basketball. Fifty pulled up and got out of the truck and said, "Yo Sun, hey!"

The two boys stopped playing and looked at him like he was crazy. They had to be round 14 or 15 years old. "Yo peep, I need some help unloading this truck – if you're trying to make some money I'll give you both two hundred dollars a piece – what's up?"

They walked up to Fifty and said, "What we got to unload?"

"Some damn furniture nigga, now do you want to get paid or what?"

"Hell yeah, we're down!"

"Then come on!"

"Where we going?"

"To my house little nigga – I'll bring you back when we're finished. Don't be scared little nigga, I'm on the up and up."

"We ain't scared; we just ain't trying to get caught up on no crazy shit."

"I feel you Sun, but it's on the real!" Fifty laughed as they jumped in the truck and went to his new town house. An hour later they were finished and Fifty was dropping them off. "Here Sun, here's an extra $50 dollars for both of you, much respect, and always keep your guards up."

"Thank you big Rob! Take care Sun." The young boy said as Fifty laughed at the alias name the young boy called him.

"Can't trust no one now-a-days." Fifty said as he drove off. He pulled up to a Circuit City at 7:30p.m. and knew that he had to put this lick down quick. As he walked in he saw Big Luke a nigga from his old high school football team.

"Oh shit, what's up Fifty? Long time no see Sun!"

"Big Luke what's up my man, it's good to see you Sun. Listen man, I got this burn out credit card that I'm trying to work, can you help me?"

"Yo Sun, you damn right! What you need?"

"The works!"

"Come on Sun, we got these new 70 inch big screen TV's in and they're like that!" Big Luke said.

"Hell yeah Sun, let me get one of them and two of them 30 inch joints too, also let me get that new hand held camcorder, and three of those DVD's and two of those JVC stereo systems, yeah; that shit's nice! I need a computer, a microwave, a new stove and refrigerator, and give me one of those 60 inch floor model TV's too. What do you want?"

"Damn Sun, I can use one of those 60 inch floor model and that Sony stereo system." Big Luke said, with an unsure look on his face!

"Cool then sun, make it happen and give me an address and number to your crib and I'll drop it off for you tonight."

"You got it sun! Let me see the card!" Fifty gave him the Master card and it went through like clock work. Big Luke had the loaders load up everything on the truck, and Fifty was off again. He pulled back up to the park and his two little helpers were sitting on the bench eating a couple of hamburgers, and fries.

"Hey Mick, Jr!" They looked and seen Fifty in the truck and ran over.

"What's up Big Rob?" Jr said.

"Yo, I need you guys help again, are you guys trying to make some more money?"

"Hell yeah Sun!" Mick yelled as they both jumped in the truck with no further questions.

After they finished unloading the stuff, Fifty dropped them back off and gave them both two hundred dollars more a piece. "Thanks hustlers!"

"Anytime Big Rob," Jr said as he put his money in his pocket and walked off.

Fifty stopped at Big Luke's apartment and his girl answered the door." Hey Tracy, my name is Fifty. Your man Big Luke asked me to drop this stuff off for him."

"Oh hi Fifty, Luke called and said that you might be stopping by. Do you need some help?"

"Yeah, you can grab some of them small boxes. Those are part of the stereo system." Fifty said as he put the big floor model 60 inch TV on the dolly and rolled it down the ramp and into Big Luke's apartment. He went back out and put the speakers and other boxes on the dolly, then rolled them into the apartment also.

"Thank you so much!"

"You're welcome, and tell Big Luke that I send my respect."

"I will!" Tracy said as Fifty left.

Fifty pulled up at his Grandmother's house at 10:45p.m. he knew that it was late, but being that it was the 4th of July, he thought she might still be up. Fifty unloaded the other 60 inch floor model TV off the truck with the dolly and rolled it to his Grandmother's door and rung the door bell.

Fifty's Grandpa answered the door and said, "Who the hell is it?"

"It's me Grandpa!" Fifty said as his grandpa turned on the porch light and peeped out of the side window. He opened up the door and said, "boy you alright?"

"Yeah Grandpa! I got a present for you and Grandma," and Fifty rolled the big TV in the house as his grandma walked out.

"Baby is that you – Is everything alright?"

"Yeah Grandma, I just wanted to bring you and grandpa a present."

"What is it baby?"

"It's a big screen TV Ma!" Grandpa said with a big smile.

"Is it stolen Baby?" Grandma asked.

Grandpa said, "who cares Ma, hell I would've stolen the damn TV myself, if I had the chance too!" Fifty started busting up knowing that his Grandpa was a TV fanatic.

"Where do you want it at pa?"

"Move that one, and put the new one right there in that spot." Fifty moved the old one and put the new one in it's spot, and took the cardboard off it. 'Now that's a damn TV!" Grandpa said as he grabbed the new remote control.

"Can you please put the other TV on the kitchen counter, so I can watch my stories in the kitchen?"

"Sure Grandma." Fifty said as he carried the old 27 inch TV in the kitchen and set it on the counter for his grandma. "There you go baby – I got to go, I love you baby." Fifty said as he gave her a kiss on the cheek and walked toward the door.

"Hey boy," Fifty looked up at this grandpa, "Thanks, and stay out of trouble!"

"I will pop's – good night now!"

"Good night Baby!"

Fifty jump back into the truck and drove back to the U-haul rental company and parked the truck out front with the keys left in the ignition, and went to jump into is car and rolled out. He made it back to his new townhouse at 11:45p.m. and was all smiles after he unloaded all of his fly gear and stuff. He put on his Povade Rolex watch, diamond chain, diamond ear rings, diamond bracelet, and both diamond rings, and smiled at his profile as he stood in the bedroom posing in the big mirror. "Once again it's on". Fifty uttered to him self as he went and started putting everything he brought up and fixing up his new dwelling.

Chapter 5
Born To Mac

It was 10:30a.m. the next day as Fifty entered the Q Motel Inn parking lot. He went to the trunk of his car and retrieved two big green hefty plastic trash bags that was full of the new ladies clothes that he just purchased from the mall with the credit cards. He went over to the young cute thick red bone hooker's motel room, and knocked on the door. She looked out the side window and had a look of surprise in her eyes as she opened the door. "Hey Red Bone!"

"Hi....!"

"Can I have a moment of your time?" Fifty said with a smile as she took one step to the side and let him walk in.

"You got to excuse my room – I was still in bed, I haven't had a chance to clean up yet," the cute hooker said as she picked up her mini skirt and boots off the floor and put them in the closet. She had on a long T-shirt and it was obvious that she was still sleeping when Fifty came over.

"Wait a minute; I'll be back, have a seat. I got to go and get myself together," she said as she rushed to the bathroom to wash her face and brush her teeth. Fifty sat down at the table were a half empty box of pizza was next to a half bottle of Remy Martin and an open can of coke. Fifty went to cut on the radio that was on top of the TV and sat back down as Mob Deep echoed threw the TV speakers.

The thick red bone hooker walked back out of the bathroom looking refreshed and awoke, as she put her long wavy black hair back into a ponytail.

Then she said, "So what's on your mind fly guy?" As she was thinking that Fifty had reconsidered and decided to come and ask her for some pussy.

"Well baby, being that you were my crimee' on that lick we put down, it's only right that I give you your cut of the profit. I wouldn't respect myself as being real if I didn't....!" Fifty said with a player smile and looked down at the two big plastic bags and said "These are for you!"

Her eyes lit up with excitement as she said "Oh no you didn't! I can't believe this." As she opened up the first bag and started pulling clothes out with excitement in here eyes. She pulled out the first big bag that had the eight Sean John ladies sweat suits and said, "Oh shit, these are like that!" Then she reached back into the bag and pulled out the bag with the five Gucci dresses. "Wow, I can't believe this; this is the finest shit that I ever had!" Then looked up at Fifty like a little kid on Christmas and said, "I can't believe that anyone would do this for me!"

"Yo Shorty, real niggas do real things! Now finish checking out your new gear baby, you know that I hooked you up proper."

She smiled as she started pulling out the Gucci boots and Gucci purse and said, "Damn, you got good taste, how did you know my size?"

"Just a luck guess, your body's very unique, so that wasn't hard and I got a little feet fetish, so I kind of noticed how small your feet was when I meet you and guessed that you were about a 7 1/2."

"You're good! The hooker said with a smile and tried on a pair of her new Gucci boots and said, "Perfect fit and they're nice and real comfortable."

"Don't you want to open up your other bag? Fifty said with a devilish look on his face.

"Hell ya,' the hooker said as she asked Fifty to help her pull off her boot, and she put her leg up so he could pull, and Fifty seen that she didn't have on any panties as her pussy lips winked at him. He looked up at her and she said, "OOOOP's my bad." And started blushing, then opened up the other plastic bag and pulled out three nice leather Sean John jackets and five nice Roc-a-wear sweaters. "Wow these are the finest clothes that I ever had." She said as she reach back into the plastic bag and pulled out ten sun dresses, seven pairs of Sean John jeans, six baby doll lingerie sets, and three Victoria secret perfumes and body bath sets. "Damn, I don't know what to say, nobody has ever gave me nothing this nice before, and I don't even know your name?

"You can call me Ice Shorty!"

"Okay Ice, pleased to meet you, my name is Nicole but my friends call me Summer."

"The pleasure mine Summer." Fifty uttered as he handed her an elegant black suede jewelry box.

"What's this?" Summer said with a surprise look on her face.

"It's just something special that I think you should have, what good is the game if it don't bless those who keep it real!" Fifty said as he handed Summer the box.

Summer opened it and her heart skipped a beat as she saw the four caret diamond bracelet smiling at her. "Oh it's beautiful Ice," she said as she walked over and gave Fifty a big hug and a kiss on the neck. And the smell of his Michael Jordan cologne was hypnotic as Summer melted into Fifty's strong embrace. "You smell good!" Summer said as she pried herself away from his body.

Fifty just smiled as he took the four caret diamond bracelet and placed it around Summer's wrist. "Now it's time for you to shine baby – play your part!" Fifty said, as he gazed in Summer's eyes and pulled her into his warm embrace and gently kissed her on the lips.

Summer was in another world as a low moan escaped her lips. "Ice I want to be your lady!" Summer uttered in a low seductive tone.

Fifty looked into her eyes and said, "baby it takes more then just looks and sex appeal to become a part of my life. I'm about money, and I don't tolerate no stupidity or disloyalty. My word is law, and I ain't got the time to be playing no silly games with women who doesn't know how to play her position in life."

"I know my position, and I'm down for my man to the fullest. Just give me a chance, you'll see!" Summer said with confidence in her tone.

"Shorty It's hard to be with a player like me, because I don't believe in jealousy and a woman in my life has to know and understand that other women do exist, and we hustle and get money together, and if I did choose to make you one of my bottom ladies, then you got to be totally about me, and thorough to the bone. You got to accept my word as law, and know that satisfying me is your number one objective. And if you can't live up to those standards, then it would only be a waste of your time, because if I sense any type of deceit, jealousy, disrespect, or disobedience, then I'll dismiss you and never respect you again."

"Baby I'm loyal to my man, and as down as they come. I'll ride for my man and take penitentiary chances for him, as well as die with my man, but I just got to know and believe in my heart that he would be down for me in the same way?"

"Do you question my realness?"

"No, you been the realest nigga that I ever met, and I'm feeling everything about you – that's why I want to choose you as my man, and give you my all, because I know that with you I have the best."

Fifty blushed vaguely at the compliment and knew that his game was on, she was trapped in his web and didn't want to get out, and it was his time to move in for the kill.

"Listen Red Bone, I'm feeling you a lot, and something tells me that you might be the down woman that I need in my life. I need a woman who's not scared to get the money, and who knows how to slang pussy and play a trick. I don't need no square bitch; I need a down bitch that's a vet. But if you think for a moment that I'll take you away from your current occupation, then you're confused about me.

I respect you for who, and what you are, and I know you know your game and would keep your man's pocket fat. But my question to you is; do you have the qualities of a bottom bitch to build me a stable of fly bitches, and be able to manage them in this game?"

"Of course baby, I can do that?" Summer said with confidence.

"Well it's only one way to see, but first tell me, what are you worth?" Summer ran over to the closet and got down on her hands and knees as she dug up under the old rug and Fifty couldn't see anything but a big fat pretty yellow ass with some fat well groomed pussy lips staring at him right in the face. Fifty grabbed his crotch and knew that that sight was too much to handle. It's been over 3 years since he had any sex, and his nuts was feeling the pressure.

Summer got up and walked over and handed Fifty a fat wad of money, "here I've been saving up, that's 8g's there." Summer said with a smile.

Fifty sat the money on the table and said, "listen Red Bone, I'm a man who likes quality things, that's why I got eyes for you, but I believe that you're a million dollar bitch, that's why I'ma give you and opportunity to show and prove, but don't ever serve me crumbs and expect me to consider it a meal. Your bracelet is worth more then 8g's."

Summer held her head down, and Fifty raised it back up." I'ma consider this a down payment, and give you a probationary period to allow you to show me the type of thorough bitch I got, if you prove yourself down for me, and our cause within the time period that I feel is appropriate, then I'ma put you where you desire to be within my life, but if not, then I'm give you back this 8g's and walk away for life – Deal?"

"Deal...!" Summer said with a small smile.

Fifty said, "Now come here and let me see what you're hiding up under that T-shirt", and Fifty pulled the T-shirt up over her head and said "Daaammn! You are flawless!" And Summer blushed as she struck a sexy pose. "What's the first rule of the game and your devotion to me" Fifty asked?

"I don't know! Is it get the money?" Summer asked, posing a question to her answer.

"Naw that's the second rule, the first rule is always satisfying your man!" They both smiled as she said "I like that rule, and she gave him a passionate kiss and started undressing him with a hungry desire.

* * * *

Fifty left Summer's motel room at 1:45p.m. and was completely satisfied. Summer was everything that a man could want in a freaky fantasy, and she knew how to use every weapon that she had to satisfy her man's desire.

Fifty took a shower with her before he departed, and left her $500 dollars so she'll have some money to get her hair and nails done and anything else a lady would need to enhance her beauty.

He told her that he had to take care of some important business, and he'll catch up with her later on. Fifty jumped in his car and gave a devilish grin as he drove off to go and make his presence felt in his comrades thoughts.

He stopped at Yayo's mother house, to go check up on her and Yayo's little sister. Fifty walked to the front door and knocked, Yayo's mother answered the door with a surprise look on her pretty face as she saw Fifty standing there.

"Hey baby, Yayo told me that you were out, but I didn't expect to see you so soon."

"Well momma Ya, I just had to come and show my love to my god brother, and bring you a little something to help you beat the hard times." Then Fifty handed her a thousand dollars.

"Oh baby, I can't accept this!"

"Mamma Ya, you know better then that! Yayo wouldn't respect me if I didn't watch over his love ones, now take it, and make sure your bills are paid and your refrigerator is full. If you need anything else, then here's my cell phone number, call me! I'ma send Yayo some money today so, don't worry about him, I got his back, o'kay?"

"O'kay baby, we love you so much, thank you for being a good man to us".

"Yo ma, you know that that's my position in life! We're a family, and we suppose to always stick together…….. feel me?"

"Yes!" Yayo mother said as she gave Fifty a big motherly hug.

"Is Tammy here?" Fifty asked referring to Yayo's little sister.

"Yeah, she's in her room – probably on the phone with her fast-ass!"

Fifty smiled and said, "Can I go talk to her?"

"Yeah, you know where her room is, go ahead." Fifty walked to Tammy's bedroom door and knocked.

"Who's there?"

"It's Fifty!"

"Who?"

"Fifty girl! Open up the door and see!"

Tammy opened up the door and said, "Oh shit, my brother's home! What's up Fifty?" as she threw her arms around his neck and gave him a big hug!

"What's up Shorty – look at you, you got big and just as fine as you want to be!" Tammy was 15 years old now, and in high school. Her small body had filled out like a young lady. "You ain't that nappy-head little girl anymore!"

"Boy please, I ain't never had no nappy-hair!" Tammy said as she ran her fingers through her long pretty hair. "Yayo said that you were out, but I didn't expect to see you so soon!"

"Yo ma, you know that I got to come and see my family, what kind of person would I be if I didn't come and see my love ones? Here, Fifty gave Tammy $500 dollars and reached in his other pocket and gave her the 3 1/2 caret diamond ankle bracelet.

"Oh Fifty, this is like that! Thank you, thank you! Tammy said as she gave Fifty a big hug and kiss on the cheek.

Fifty kneeled down and clipped it around her ankle and said, "This represent success, so I want to see you strive with every step you take, to be successful in life. That means studying hard and getting good grades to show the world that you're smarter then most, and don't let no nigga's or sex control your life. Wear protection if you fuckin with them niggas, and always strive to have a career in life, not just a bullshit 9 to 5 job! Do you understand where I'm coming from?"

"Yes....!"

"Good, because your family believes in you, and need you to step your game up, so you can help us open up the door to success. You got what it takes, but you just got to believe in yourself, and understand your cause and position in life. You can be like the rest of the young fast ghetto girls who end up getting pregnant and trapped in this ghetto maze, or you can go the different route, and strive toward a promising career, and chase success. It's up to you and now is the time to decide and take your position in life. We love you and are down for you, but you must choose your place and fate in life. You feel me?"

"Yeah Fifty, I feel you and I'ma give myself a reality check and see what I really want out of life, O'kay?"

"That's my little sis! I love you girl, and if you need me, then call me, here's my number!"

"O'kay thank you big bro!"

"You're welcome Shorty!"

Fifty turned and walked out of the room and momma Ya was sitting on the couch listening to the jewels that Fifty dropped on Tammy, and she said, "Thank you baby, she needed that!" and gave Fifty a big hug.

Fifty said, "That's what family's for," and smiled as he walked out the front door.

Fifty jumped in his car and headed straight for the post office and brought five $200 dollars postal money orders, and sent Yayo, Power, Black, Little Chucky and Big Caesar each one with a card that read, "Got your backs – half dollar!"

Then he sent them all two paper-back books and a different urban magazine a piece.

Fifty left the book store and decide to hit up Red Lobster and treat himself to a fat lobster and king crab leg dinner, and as he was going down a residential street, he saw a bad ass black 600 Benz coup sitting on some 20 inch Astanta Rims, as Fifty past by, he saw Mario an old Puerto Rican reverie that shot up his old 5.0 mustang back in the days, and hit Big Game in the shoulder and arm.

"Look what I've stumbled across," Fifty said to himself as he pulled his car over to the curve and parked.

He watched Mario hit the alarm to his car, and walked up and took his keys and opened up the front door to his house.

"Damn, this is a needle in a hay stack." Fifty muttered to himself as he sat in his car and contemplated his next move.

Everyone knew that Mario was ballin hard, Fifty got word in the pen about it, but Mario didn't fuck with to many people, so niggas couldn't get a good trace on him.

Now out of the blue, Fifty turned down a nice residential street and stumbled across Mario as he was walking into his house.

"It might be his stash house," Fifty thought and looked around the neighborhood to see if he could spot any noisy neighbors. But, everything looked quiet and peaceful.

It was 4:15p.m. and Fifty was starving, but his hunger for revenge and money was a lot stronger, so he took off his Sean John sweat coat that he had on, and took off his T-shirt and wife beater, than put his T-shirt and sweat coat back on, and stuffed his wife beater in his sweat coat pocket and got out of his car and causally walked over to Mario's house, and made his way down along-side the house as he looked through each window.

Mario neighbors must've still been at work, because their house was too quiet. Fifty went around the back and seen Mario talking on the phone and counting stacks of money at his living room table.

Fifty looked around and saw what he was looking for, then took the wife beater T-shirt out of his pocket and tied it around his nose, mouth and chin of his face, then fixed his New York starter hat down low over his eyes.

Fifty waited until Mario got off the phone and then picked up a big stone that Mario had laying around his flower garden as decoration, and Fifty threw it right through Mario's big sliding glass window, and ran through the broken glass window with his big black 45 automatic in hand without getting a scratch.

"Put your damn hands up fool before I blow your damn head off."

"O'kay, o'kay, don't shoot, don't shoot!" Mario said as he put his hands in the air.

"You know what time it is – you son-of-a-bitch get your punk ass on the got damn floor, and you better do it slow!" Fifty ordered.

"O'kay, o'kay!" Mario said as he layed on the floor.

"Fifty went over and searched him and took a big ass desert Eagle from out of Mario's waste band. Fifty looked at the big desert Eagle and was glad that Mario froze-up, and didn't get to it in time. Fifty said, "Cross your damn legs and put your hands behind your head, fool you know the position". Mario quickly complied and Fifty saw the fat diamond ring, bracelet, chain and Rolex watch that Mario had on. "Take off your jewelry! Who else is here?"

"No one, just me." Mario said nervously as he took off all of his jewelry and sat it by his head so Fifty could reach it.

"How much money is that?" Fifty said as he picked up the jewelry and put it in his pocket.

"It's $60,000 dollars!"

"Fifty grabbed the phone cord and quickly tied up Mario's hands, and started putting the money back in the sports bag. "Now you can live through this day or you can die today, it's up to you. Now where is the safe and dope at?"

It's in the bedroom closet-you can have it, just please don't kill me man!"

"As long as you give me what I came for, then you can live, now get up and let's go to your safe." Fifty grabbed the back of his shirt and drugged him to his feet and walked him to the back room where the safe and dope was at. "Lay down right here," Fifty ordered as he laid Mario halfway into the closet. "What's the combination?"

"6-10-7....!"

Fifty opened the safe and saw stacks of money neatly lined up. "How much is this?"

"Around a hundred thousand dollars!"

"Fifty grabbed the medium size Gucci suit case and opened it, and it had kilo's of cocaine in it. Fifty counted 12 bricks and said "where is the rest?"

"That's all of it!"

Fifty grabbed another Gucci sports bag and it was empty, so he put the money in it. Then he looked around the closet and found a Tec 9 and an AR-15, and grabbed a black leather trench coat and wrapped them up in it. Fifty looked around through the dressers with a towel over his hands and found a big fat 357 magnum. He looked around and grabbed a pillow from off the bed and said, "Yo Mario, tell my nigga Big Game that I send my love." Mario eyes got big as he looked up and recognized Fifty right before Fifty put the pillow over his head and blow Mario brains out.

Fifty grabbed the bag with the dope and took a kilo out with the towel and put it under the mattress, then grabbed the two Gucci bags and leather trench and walked out of the bedroom, as he retrieved the other sports bag and stone on his way out. He took off the wife beater from around his face, and then walked out nonchalant the same way he went in. The streets was still quiet and empty, as Fifty walked out to his car and throw the bags in the passenger seat, then he drove off looking through his rear-view mirror to see if anyone was watching. Fifty swooped around the corner and got the stuff out of the passenger seat, and put it all up in the trunk of his car in case he got pulled over. Then he laughed to himself as he drove back to his townhouse half paranoid.

When Fifty made it back home, he brung all of the bags in with the guns, then went to jump in the shower to wash the gun powder residue off. After that, he went out to his car and wiped down the steering wheel and took the clothes, towel, and stone that he used to put his lick down with, and got rid of them all in different locations. Then he went to Mc Donald's drive thru and grabbed him two super size value packs and went back home to count his come up.

Fifty hit Mario for $155,000 dollars and 11 kilos of cocaine, as well as around 50 to 60 thousand dollars worth of Jewelry and some nice guns. "Pay backs a bitch!" Fifty said as he laughed and put on his new leather Sean John jacket, and went to go do some shopping at the supermarket for food and needed necessities.

Fifty had three full baskets of groceries as he went to the counter, and the old white casher looked up at Fifty and said

"I'ma need some assistance on register 3 please." And Fifty just laughed and shook his head.

After he took the food home, he went to the mall and went into Bullocks and brought some expensive bed sheets and blankets, and microwave bowls, pots, pans, silverware, and dishes, then he grabbed some towels and bathroom supplies.

Then headed back home to hook his spot up, after he finished he looked around his plushed out spot and smiled as he put his Tupac, 'All Eyes On Me' CD in the stereo system, and bumped it at a low mellow tone, as he pulled out two kilo's and started putting his cook game down.

He knew that it was time to take it to a whole nother level, so he had to make sure that his young gorilla crew could eat good too.

He took the kilos and just cooked up 36 ounces off each one of them, so he had 72 ounces of rock cocaine that wasn't cut and stretched like the way Red serve it, cause he know that his little gorilla crew would take all of Red's workers clientele, once the base heads get a taste of the good shit. Fifty sipped his glass of Hennessy as he contemplated his next move, and then smiled.

* * * *

Summer was the hottest thang on the hoe stroll, as she strutted up and down the street stopping traffic both ways. She had her hair cut into a short sexy Toni Braxton hair cut, and it showed off her beautiful facial features like a top paid model, as she switched her big round fat ass in the tight mini-dress out fit. She been on the strip for only four hours and already made $900 dollars. She laughed as the old white man pulled up in the new white Jag and said "Whatever your price is honey, I'll pay it!"

"Summer said, "I seen this new out fit I like but it cost $350 dollars."

"You're worth it, and I'ma make sure you can afford it"! The man said.

"Well it sounds good, but I only got 30 minutes to spare." Summer said, with a sexy pose and seductive smile.

"I only need 20 minutes, beautiful!" The old man said as he grabbed his crotch.

"Let me see what you're working with to make sure that I'm not being played." Summer said as the old white man pulled out his little 6 inch pink dick, and shook it. "Oooowow! You got a nice one! Pull up in the motel right there, and we can go to my room and play!" Summer said with a sexy smile as she stuck out her tongue. And the old white man complied with no hesitation. Summer kept an extra room for her tricks, because she didn't want to lay her head where she did her dirt at. She thought about her man 'Ice,' and smiled as she walked up to the trick and took him into her world of fantasy and pleasure.

Chapter 6
It's On Again

It was Friday morning and Fifty woke up hyped feeling $155 thousand dollars richer, not including the 11 keys of cocaine. It was a pretty good start to a new beginning, and Fifty knew that he had to make calculated moves. He jumped out of the silk sheets and started the day off with his regular work out routine, because he knew that this was the time that he did his best thinking. After his work out, he showered and got dressed to impress. He threw on his fly red and gray Roc-a-wear sweat suit with the suede patches, and some fresh new red, white and gray Jordan's. He grabbed the duffle bag full of money that he had counted and separated, and was off on a mission.

His first stop was the exotic car dealership on Suphtin Blvd that his old acquaintance owned. He pulled up on the exotic car lot and seen exactly the fetish to his desire, a brand new 1999 black Range Rover with tint and dark gray leather guts. Fifty looked up and seen his old acquaintance walking up with a big smile. "What's up Poppy!" The old fat Puerto Rican man said as he walked up looking like he was connected to the mob.

"Mocho my old friend, how are you doing Sun?" Fifty said.

"Better then most my friend, It's been a long time Poppy - looked at you, you've got big! Full of muscles, you been away yeah?" Mocho said, as he looked at Fifty with a broken grin.

"Yeah my friend, I had to pay my dues to the white man, he don't like to see us doing good!"

"You right about that my friend! You got to be smart Poppy...... don't trust nobody!"

"I hear you my friend – I came to do business…. How much for the Range?"

"This one is real nice, brand new, but young man come to me and buy it, put a big down payment and three weeks later, pow, dead! He put miles on it, so I sell to you for good price, good sound system and everything, listen? Mocho cut on the sound system and the four 12" woffers awoke with an enticing roar. Fifty smiled knowing that Mocho knows how much blacks like load music, so he's using the sound system to make his sale pitch.

"The system sounds alright, but brings to much attention in a since, if you know what I mean?"

Mocho just nodded his head knowing that Fifty just put him in catch 22. "If you don't like, I can remove it for you–that's no problem!"

"Well my friend, it's no big deal, how much as is?" Fifty said as Mocho smiled.

"I tell you what Poppy, you give me sixty thousand dollars and it's yours!"

Fifty knew that that was a good deal especially considering that it was still brand new and had an eight thousand dollar sound system already in it.

"That deals just for you Poppy!" Mocho added.

"O'kay listen Mocho, I'll give you sixty thousand dollars cash today, but you have to carry the finance for me, and hook it up so them white people won't be knocking on my door, and you carry the insurance for the first year."

"Don't worry Poppy, I got you! I'll carry the paperwork and hook everything up for you. No IRS nothing! And if you get caught-up and need me to resale, I'll do it for you Poppy for only five percent of what I sale for, and send you the rest. If police take it, I'll go get it back for you, we do good business! O'kay!"

"Deal......!" Fifty said, as he went to the trunk of his car and grabbed the black duffle bag full of money-and followed Mocho into the office.

After Fifty purchased the truck, he had Mocho have one of his workers to follow him in his Cutless as he went straight to the Rim Shop, and brought some 20" chrome star Giavonta Rims and low profile tires to go with his new pimp mobile. He told the rim shop manager that he'll pick his truck up later, then dropped Mocho worker back off and gave him $50 dollars and then proceeded to his next destination.

"Welcome to Kutlers Law Office, how may I help you Sir?"

"Yes, is Mr. Kutler in!"

"Do you have an appointment Sir?"

"No I don't Maam!"

"What's your name Sir?"

"Tell him Fifty is here to see him."

"Fifty; as in half dollar?"

"Yes!"

"O'kay, just a moment Sir!" The secretary called into Mr. Kutler office and said, excuse me Mr. Kutler, you have a gentleman here, by the name of Fifty that's requesting to see you."

"Yes, as in a half dollar!"

"Sure!"

"Sir, he said he'll see you, please follow me" and the cute blond hair secretary escorted Fifty to Mr. Kutler office and opened the door for Fifty to walk in.

"Mr. Fifty, hi my name is Mr. Kutler!"

"Please to meet you," Fifty said as they shook hands.

"Have a seat, and what can I do for you?"

"Well Mr. Kutler, I hear that you are one of the best on state appeals, and I got a close comrade that's incarcerated in Clinton State Prison who desires your services."

"Is that right? What kind of case is it?"

"Drug, assault, attempted murder! From what I understand someone got shot and pistol whipped, and the person who did it got away, but a witness gave a name that they thought the assailant looked like, and the police kicked in my man's door to arrest him, and found a kilo of dope. They railroaded him in trial, even after the eye witness said that he didn't look like the man that she seen doing the shooting. So my man got a bad rap, and need a good voice to plead his case on an appeal. Now my question to you is, how much do you charge for an appeal?"

"Well I charge $12,000 dollars for an appeal, and an additional $8,000 dollars if I get a retrial and have to represent him in those proceedings too.

"O'kay now listen, I'ma give you $25,000 dollars for you to represent him and additional $5,000 dollars to retain you as my attorney just in case I may need your assistance in the future.

"We can do that!" Kutler said with a smile.

"Tell me, do you deal with cases regarding prostitution?"

"I'm one of the best!"

"Good, because I have some lady friends who's are prominent in the field!" Fifty said with a devilish grin.

"Do they work out of an escort service?"

"Should they?"

"It's best if you want to put some added protection on yourself for criminal liability if they get busted. This way even if they try to tell on you, then you have them under contractual agreement saying that it's forbidden for them to have sex with any clients while working at your escort service. Also, you can put your profit in a bank and pay taxes on it, because you're considered a legitimate business now."

"How much will it cost to start an escort service?"

"I can draw up the paper work for the company, and get you the business license and then draw up the contractual agreement applications, and have you registered and up and running by Monday for $3,000 dollars."

"Deal! Make it happen!"

"Do you have a name for your business?"

"Call it 50/7 connection!"

"That's different!" Kutler said as he raised his eye brow curiously.

"Here!" Fifty started pulling out a wad of money from every pocket and counted out $33,000 dollars and gave the attorney Yayo name and case number, as well as Momma Ya's number.

"The attorney said, "I see that you come prepared," When he saw all the cash, then he wrote out a receipt and hand it to Fifty.

Fifty knew that Kulter was one of the best criminal attorney's in the game, because his name was ringing all through the pen as a convict attorney. And if anyone could help Yayo get out, then cut 'em lose Bruce' would definitely be the one! Fifty shook Mr. Kutlers hand as he was about to go, and Mr. Kutler stopped him and wrote down his cell phone number on the back of a business card, and give it to Fifty and said, "call me anytime day or night"

"I will." Fifty said as he grabbed three more business cards and departed.

* * * *

It was 3:30p.m. when Fifty turned into the parking lot of the Guy Brewer projects. Little G-nut, Ra, and Baby Tank were all kicking it in the cut getting their serve on, when they spotted Fifty pull-up and park. All of them walked over to greet their comrade. "What's up young gorillas?" Fifty said, as he gave his young comrades their secret hand shake.

"Nothing Rad, just slangin, bangin, and hangin!" Little G-nut said.

Fifty laughed, "Ya'll getting money?"

"Trying, we waiting for this nigga Cubin Mike from the Bronx to come by and bring our money for this nigga!"

Fifty eyes deemed at the mention of Cubin Mikes name, and then he said, "What nigga?"

Ra looked at Baby Tank and Little G-nut and said, "Let's show him!" As they all looked at Fifty, and Ra said, "follow us!" They walked 30 yards away to an old 74 Buick and popped the trunk and a tall skinny man was in the trunk blind-folded and beat-up, tide and gagged.

"What the fuck is up with this? Fifty asked as Ra closed the trunk.

"Yo Sun, this foul ass nigga snitched on Cubin Mike's man, and it's a bounty on his head."

"Is that right, how much?" Fifty asked!

"$5000 dollars Sun!" Baby Tank said, as Cubin Mike pulled up in a Black Lincoln navigator truck with two other cars trailing behind him. Fifty looked at Cubin Mike as he walked up with two of his crew with him, and Cubin Mike eyes kind of lit up when he notice Fifty standing their with the youngsters.

"Fifty, what's up my friend, long-time no see! Look Tito, it's Fifty!" Fifty looked at Tito and smiled, then seen the big scar on Tito face that the 3.80 bullet made when Fifty shot him way back in the days when both their crews was beefing over some territory. "Yo my friend, the past is gone; we live a new day today. No hard feelings!"

The youngsters looked at Fifty and seen that he had his hand clenching the butt of his 45 automatic, and they instantly did the same.

"Yo Sun, I'm not trippin, we was kids then, and hungry for the same food, now we're grown and striving to succeed!"

"Yes my friend, that's all." Cubin Mike said, then turned to the youngsters and said, "I heard that you had a present for me?"

Ra looked at Fifty, and Fifty nodded, then Ra opened-up the trunk and the smell of shit hit the air, "Yes," Cubin Mike said, "you knew that I would catch you huh! We have a place waiting for you in hell, you rat piece of shit!"

Ra closed the trunk and handed Cubin Mike the keys and said, "When you finish with the car, then burn it, it's a G-ride!"

"O'kay my little friend, Cubin Mike said as he dug in his pocket and pulled out the 5g's.

Fifty held up his hand and said "Keep it, this one's on us! Snitches fuck up the game for the real, and it wouldn't be dignified for them to except money for keeping it real. Our integrity is what we hold strong too! Therefore, it was our pleasure, and a gift to you and your comrades."

Cubin Mike was looking Fifty in the eyes and said, "Men of honor and integrity deserve the utmost respect, if you ever need me for anything then just call, and if it's within my power then I'll be there!"

Respect Sun!" Fifty said as they shook hands. Cubin Mike shook all of the youngsters' hands, and Fifty looked up and seen Tito extending his hand and Fifty smiled as they shook hands too.

"Tito! Drive the bucket we'll follow you!"

"O'kay," Tito said as he jumped into the Buick and they all left out following behind the car headed for hell.

"Damn! There go our come up!" Baby Tank said as he shook his head and they all looked at Fifty.

"Yo Sun, there's things more important then a couple of dollars in this game, and that's a man's integrity and self respect! If you pride yourself on being a real man then you got to stand on some principles and values. This builds respect among men and sometimes that's something that can be considered priceless!"

"Yeah but where starving Sun, we could've used that 5g's to get on, and still had our respect for snatching the snitch up for him. Don't that amount for something?" Ra asked!

"Yeah it do, but you wouldn't have the Cubin cocaine connection that Cubin Mike offers to his close associated. That nigga got parts of the Bronx on lock, but he only sells big weight!"

"So how can that help us when we're broke?" Little G-nut questioned with a sarcastic look on his face.

"You don't plan on being broke all of your career, did you? Fifty asked as they looked at each other with a stupid look on their face. "Do ya'll have a place where we can kick it and talk in private?"

"Yeah, we can go to our apartment!" Ra said.

"Who lives there with you?"

"Nobody we live alone! Ra answered.

"Is that right, well come on and let me show you what I got in my trunk!" Fifty said with a devilish grin. The youngsters looked at each other puzzled, and then followed Fifty to the trunk of the Cutless. Fifty popped the trunk and looked at Baby Tank and said, "Yo Sun, grab the leather trench coat!"

"Yo, what is this? Oh shit – Yo kid, its some choppers." Tank said with excitement as Fifty smiled and grabbed the brown paper bag and looked at Ra and said, "lead the way young Rade!"

When they entered into the youngsters apartment Fifty seen that it was clean and neat, but had some old worn out furniture that barely was holding up. Fifty sat on the couch and dumped the ounces of rock cocaine out on the old table, and the youngsters eyes was in shock as they gazed at all the dope.

"Damn Sun, how much is that?" Ra asked.

"It's 72 ounces!" Fifty said with a smile

"Yo Sun, I ain't never seen that much dope." Little G-nut said.

"Me either," said Baby Tank as he put the trench coat on the rug.

"Ya'll ready to ball, or what Sun? Fifty asked. "Yo, you damn right we're ready!" said Little G-nut as him and Baby Tank gave each other dap.

"Yo peep Sun, I'ma give ya'll 18 ounces a piece to get you started, and all you got to bring me is $500 dollars on every ounce."

"That's love!" Ra said.

"But, all you can sell is to smokers, that means, don't give them other niggas no double ups or nothing. We're about to corner the market and take over this area. You guys ought to make at lease $1,500 dollars off each ounce, which will give you a profit of $18,000 dollars after every sack. Therefore, it's no way you can loose. And it's that cavie, so once the smokers get a taste of your product, then they all are going to flock to ya'll and that nigga Red workers is going to be left holding that bullshit that they got. Now this is going to cause a little bit of conflict of interest, so that's where the big guns come in at, to make sure that a nigga don't get out of line, or get this game twisted." Fifty put on his brownie gloves and picked up the AR-15 high power rifle and clicked the info red beam, and a red dot appeared on the wall.

"That's ill." Ra said.

"So is this." Said Baby Tank, as he grabbed the Mac 10 submachine gun with his brownie gloves on, and inspected it.

"It's about to go down big and I need you three to be able to hold this down for the crew. Also, I'ma promote ya'll to lieutenant's and give ya'll the power to recruit some young down and thorough niggas."

"That's what I'm taking about!" Little G-nut said.

"But ya'll got to represent this game right! All ya'll little soldiers got to be thorough and down for the cause, and you got to instill principles and values in them. None of that stupid unnecessary dumb shit. Running around shooting base heads over crumbs and doggin' them out. They're your clientele, so you got to treat them with respect and as humans, so they will enjoy coming around and spending their hard earned money with you. And if them jealous hearted niggas try to disrespect you, or fuck up your hustle, then don't hesitate to punish them. It's real in this game, so don't take it for granted, when your pockets is fat and bitches is jockin your swagger, because you got a fly whip and is doing big thangs. Also, find you guy's another spot away from the hood, so you can hide your ends at, and somewhere good that you can stash the bulk of your dope at. Like pay the rent for one of those old ladies in the project every month so that you can keep your dope hid in their spot, and tell them keep it a secret because your business ain't no one else!' You feel me?"

"Hell yeah Sun, we feel you man, and we appreciate you keeping it 'G' with us. You're the realest big homie we got! Ra said.

"Fo real…!" Little G-nut agreed.

"Yo, what about Juice!" Baby Tank asked.

"Oh, you know that I got him covered too, that's my little Gorilla, I put him down, and he's as down and as real as they get. I'ma give him the same as ya'll, as a matter of fact, call him so I can put him up on this game too!"

Baby Tank went to call him and Juice was knocking on the apartment door in three minutes flat. Fifty gave them all their first sack and laced Juice with the "take over game plan." And the rest was in full effect as the youngsters went right to work. Fifty asked Juice to roll with him and Fifty drove to pick up his Range Rover at the rim shop.

"Yo Sun, you the coldest nigga I know!" Juice said as he seen the brand new Range Rover sitting on chrome 20" Giavonta rims.

Fifty jumped in his truck and had Juice to follow him over to his grandmothers house to park the Cutless, and then they rolled back to the projects so Fifty could drop Juice back off so he could get his hustle on.

"Now that's what I call some fly shit!" Little G-nut said as the three youngsters walked up to Fifty's new Range Rover.

"Yo, you ain't lying Sun, that muthafucka's ill kid!" Ra said.

"Don't worry nigga; you'll have one in a month, if that's what you want! Just stack your money, and get your hustle on. I'ma make sure that we eat good, believe that!"

"Yo Rade, we believe you – I've already sold a half ounce and it only been about two hours. I ain't never seen so many smokers hit me up that quick." Baby Tank said.

"Me either! I didn't think these smokers had that kind of money. They love this shit," Little G-nut said.

"Yo, here I go, "Ra said as he went to go serve a smoker.

"Yo Sun, I got to go – I got some business to take care of. Call me when you need me!"

"Alright Sun – catch you later!" Juice said as Fifty pulled off beating Biggie Smalls song 'Get Money'! And the 12" woofers was acting a fool as the bass hit.

* * * *

Fifty stopped by Yayo mother's house and gave her the attorney's business card and a copy of the receipt that the attorney gave him. She was in tears and held Fifty in her strong embrace as she thanked him.

"Hey mommy Ya, we're family, that's what we do!" Fifty uttered as he handed her an envelope with 5g's in it, and another one with $2,500 in it for Tammy.

Momma Ya said, We love you so much baby, and don't you ever forget that, we're here if you should ever need us – O'kay!"

"I won't forget Ma – if you talk to Yayo give him my cell phone number and tell him that I'ma be shooting him some more money this weekend."

"O'kay baby, I'll tell him, bye!"

"Bye, bye momma Ya!"

When Fifty left momma Ya's house it was 9:00p.m., and the moon was out and shinning it's light on the party.

Fifty went straight to the Q Motel Inn and as he was pulling up, he seen Summer walking down the street looking like a runway model with her fly new hair cut.

Fifty beeped and Summer looked and seen the black Range Rover with tinted windows and chrome rims, and kept walking thinking it was a pimp trying to get at her.

She knew the rules of the game, that a hoe isn't suppose to talk to a pimp, or he'll try to claim her or take her trap money. Therefore, she just ignores them when they try to holla, so she won't bring any unnecessary problems to herself. She knew that every pimp was after her, they even be trying to send their hoes at her to try to influence and persuade her to get with their pimp. But, Summer always rejected them too, and now only one nigga makes a difference in her life, and that's her Ice!

Fifty beeped the horn again and rolled down his passenger side window and said, "Damn Ma, is that how you treat your man?"

Summer looked over and seen Fifty and said, "Oh baby, I'm sorry – I didn't know that it was you. I thought that it was another pimp trying to get at me."

"Yo, don't be sorry – I don't mess with nothing sorry baby! Get in!" Fifty said as Summer excitedly jumped into the passenger side, and lend over and kissed him on the cheek.

"Hi daddy, I missed you!" Summer said as Fifty smiled and drove off.

"I missed you too baby and I came to get you to take you out to dinner with me." Fifty said as he pulled into the motel parking lot. Summer showed how excited she was by her smile and body language.

"So, I want you to go get fly for your man, so we can paint the town!"

"O'kay daddy! I love this truck; you're doing damn thang in this!" She said, as they got out of the Range Rover and walked into the motel room.

"Give me a minute – I got to jump in the shower because I've been hustling for my man," she said as she pulled off her dress and stood naked in her high heels as she walked over to the closet and got on her hands and knees and grabbed her money from her secret stash spot underneath the rug, and Fifty just stared at that big pretty yellow ass and sexy pussy lips as they enticed him from a distance.

"Damn baby, I love it when you do that!" Fifty said as she sat a wad of bills on the table for him.

And said, "Well I guess that I got to do it more often," and smiled!

"How much is that? Fifty asked.

"Its sixteen hundred dollars and I still got some of the money that you gave me if you need it?" Summer said with a proud smile.

"O'kay, I see that I got a thoroughbred on my team!" She blushed at his compliment. "And I love your new hair cut and you're doing the most with that style. It compliments those pretty brown eyes and your beautiful facial features."

"I'm glad that you like it baby, I wanted to look my best for my man, because I know that I got a real man on my team, and I'm a reflection of you, so I got to keep it fly." Summer said with a pretty smile.

"You damn right! Now go get yourself ready because I'm starving!"

"Okay daddy, I'll be ready soon, give me ten minutes. Summer said, as she switched her big pretty yellow ass in the bathroom.

Fifty grabbed his dick and said, now this is going to be a good life," and smiled as he poured himself a shot of Remy Martin.

* * * *

"Yo Sun, this shit is selling like crazy!" Little G-nut said, as he was chopping up another ounce.

"I know Sun! Smoker Dam said that we got the best shit in the hood kid." Ra added.

"I sold one and a half ounces already and it's still early, we're going to kill the game with this Sun!"

"I told you guys that when Fifty got out, we was going to get money. My nigga's about it for real – watch ya'll ain't seen nothing yet, we're about to take this whole project over Sun. I'm telling you, Fifty's a master mind as a hustler, and he's a boss gorilla! You nigga's will see! Whatever you do, don't try to cross him, or deceive him, because he'll make your mother kill you." Juice said, as he kicked game to his young crew.

"Word?" Baby Tank said.

"You damn right – either you're down with him all the way, or you're in the way! He's a fuckin real gorilla, it's in our nature to watch over our own kind, and destroy any-other animal who tries to pose a threat to us. So you better believe that it's about to get ugly around here – so keep your game tight and gun close, because to many other animals is eating and shitting in our domain! Believe this Sun!"

"Yo, I'm with it Sun – I'm down for the gangsta' shit!" Little G-nut added.

"Me too! Fuck these buster's, they been trying to play us short anyway, now we're the Gorillas with the big nuts around here. And if they want war, I'll take them fuckin cock- roaches to war!" Baby Tank said as he gave them this best scar face impression.

Chapter 7
Hate the Game, Not the Player

Fifty and Summer pulled up at a popular soul food restaurant on Linden Boulevard that everybody goes too. They got out of the Range Rover looking like a million bucks, as they walked hand and hand into the restaurant.

Summer was wearing her favorite new Red Gucci dress with some nice Red Gucci boots to match, and Fifty just put on his big leather Roc-a-wear jacket over his new leather and suede Roc-a-wear sweat suit, and kept it gangsta' but fly. Together they turned heads like celebrities.

The waitress seated them at a back table and all eyes were on them. Some bitches whispered and smiled, and you seen some niggas look real surprised when they saw Fifty walk by.

He had a pretty good and popular reputation around the city and those who knew him, knew that he was a true hustler and gangsta', and the women loved his swagger. So his game was well recognized, and the secret was out, Fifty was home from the pen!

"Damn Shorty, I'm feeling your lovely vibe tonight, you walk like you belong next to me." Summer blushed as Fifty continue to kick his game.

"When I first seen you, I thought that you was just the average bitch who didn't have no game or finesse about herself. You know the type – born with a lovely face and nice body, with nothing else to compliment it. But I see now, that I could've judged you wrong. You're a woman of substance who knows her position in life, and who's not afraid of the challenges that life tends to inflict on the unfortunate.

You're very similar to me, because you know how to make your own opportunities in life, and take advantage of the weak and ignorant sucka's of the world. You are a princess looking for her prince to come and fulfill her desire for love and companionship. I can see it in your pretty eyes, your soul don't lie! But, I truly wonder how deep is your love, and devotion? I know that you've been hurt and deceived in life before, you gave your heart to a sucka and he betrayed your thoughts and emotions. Did this destroy the opportunity for a real man to come into your life, and enjoy the pleasures of your all and all?

Can I trust you?

Will you deceive me?

I'm a man of the night, a street hustler, the one that people label a thug and a gangsta'. I'm a product of my up bringing, and a curse to my heart, because it's hard for me to love, but what I love, I love unconditionally! I'm a man of honor, pride, dignity, loyalty and respect, and I look for and expect the same from all those I commit myself to in life. I don't tolerate disloyalty. So I expect the best out of my companions. My word is law, and if my companion cannot accept this, then she has the free will to go! I don't believe in keeping a woman hostage. If a woman cannot abide by my rules and authority, then I will dismiss her. Because in the game that I'm in your soul is your only collateral, and if you make one foolish mistake then it could easily be game over! Even my ladies got to be on top of their game, because a nigga will try to hurt you, to get at hurting me! That's why I play for keeps. So; if you desire to become a part of my life, you must know that the stakes is high, and the game is real. Niggas will kill over little or nothing, and a prayer can't stop a bullet. So either you're totally down with this game, or you need to find yourself a different kind of nigga to be with."

Fifty kicking-game was interrupted when the waitress brought their food.

"Would you guys like any thing else? The waitress asked after setting their plates down.

"No Maam, this is fine for now!"

"O'kay if you need me then just wave!"

"O'kay, thank you!" Fifty said as the waitress left.

"Listen honey," Summer begin, I know and understand what type of man I got in my life, and I've searched for you for years, and now I'm glad that I have finally found you. I don't care what we have to do to get there, I just want to be by your-side, and be considered your main bitch when we make it. I'm not afraid of taking penitentiary chances, because I believe if I do fall, then you will make sure that my needs is met and be there for me, like I would do for you, if ever you got caught up. 'Knock on wood!'

Summer said, as she knocked on the table. "So whatever you need me to do, then I'm down for you to the fullest, just don't ever dog me out please, cause I believe in you, and I'm caught up over you," Summer said as she rubbed Fifty's hand from across the table.

"I feel you Shorty, and something in my heart tells me that you're sincere. But only time will tell! Nevertheless, I'ma give you the benefit of the doubt, and give you chance and opportunity that you're asking for, but if you ever try to deceive my thoughts, or lack in your game, or show jealousy toward another bitch, then I'ma walk away. I promise that!"

"Honey you don't have to worry about that, I know my position in your life, and I would always be your bottom lady. You can believe that!"

"I believe you baby, but you got a lot to prove." Fifty said as they shared a good laugh and a kiss.

After they ate, they went to a popular night club and got their groove on. It's been 3 years since Fifty had partied and he was getting it on, as he had one of the baddest bitches in the place. They danced for a half hour straight, and then went to the bar to get some drinks.

While they were enjoying each-other vibes Fifty notice and old rival of his past, walking over to them with a crew of 3 big buff niggas.

"Damn!" Fifty said as he looked at Summer and said, "Do you know how to drive?"

"Yeah baby of course!"

"Cool here," Fifty gave her his keys and said, "you might better meet me at the truck and get my heat from under the seat for me."

"Why what's up baby?" Summer said as a nigga walked up and said, "What's up Fifty-long time no see!" Jaru said as him and his crew walked up.

"Not long enough Ja, what you still mad about that little stab wound I gave you?" Fifty said with a sinister laugh.

"A little, but little wounds heal pretty good; it's just the big ones that don't heal that good." Jaru said.

"Well I know that this one is going to bother you a lot" Fifty said as he socked Jaru in the eye and knocked him down.

Jaru crew rushed Fifty as Fifty started throwing a fury of combinations at his attackers. Fifty knocked the first one out, and dropped the second one, but the third one grabbed Fifty around the mid section trappin one of his arms as Jaru got up and socked Fifty three good times in the face.

Summer saw her man caught up, and grabbed a bottle from off a table nearby, and hit the third member who was holding Fifty across the head shattering the bottle and knocking him out cold.

Fifty seen that and rushed Jaru with a fury of punches, dropping him to the ground, and Summer slapped the second dude in the face with a long neck Budweiser bottle and the impact knock the dude two front teeth out as he fell back and grabbed his mouth.

He said, "Bitch I'ma kill you!"

And before he could attack back, the bouncers at the club was all over them, Fifty, Jaru, and the rest of the crew as they were rushed to the ground.

Summer slipped out during the commotion and went out to the truck and started it, then pulled out in-front of the club, and placed Fifty's big black 45 automatic on her lap, then she saw two big buff bouncers drugged Fifty out by his leather jacket.

Summer jumped out of the truck and pointed the gun at the bouncers and said "you better let him go muthafuckas, or I'ma shoot the shit out of you!"

They hurried up and dropped Fifty and held their hands up as they walked backwards.

Fifty laughed and ran over and grabbed the gun as the bouncer was walking backwards quicker, and Fifty said, "Get in baby lets roll." Then they jumped back into the truck and punched out.

Summer asked, "Are you o'kay?"

Fifty laughed out loud again and said, "Of course Shorty, with a down lady like you by my side I can't lose." Then Summer smiled as Fifty held her hand to his lips and kissed the back of it.

"I told you that I'm down for my man, they're lucky I didn't have a gun on me, or I would've shot all of them busters. But you handled your business daddy, you was swinging and dropping them left and right. It was just too many of them."

"Fuck them busta's they can't fuck with me, I'ma real silver back gorilla!" Fifty laughed as he pulled up into a 7-11 store and said, "I'll be back, I got to grab me some ice for my face and hand. You want something?"

"Yeah, grab me a cranberry juice and a snicker."

"Got you!" Fifty said as he went into the 7-11 and grabbed the things he needed. He grabbed two 6 packs of magnums, some lubrication, baby oil, soap, deodorant, two tooth brushes and some tooth paste, ice, jolly ranchers, candy bars, chips, gum, juice and a 12 pack of Millers. He jumped back into the truck and headed for the Marriot hotel. He got the suite with the Jacuzzi and see through shower, and it was on and poppin. As soon as they walked into the room Fifty sat down the bags and looked over at Summer with a lustful grin and said "Strip!" She smiled and didn't hesitate as Fifty walked up and said "what the first rule of devotion?"

She smiled and bent down on her knees, and pulled his dick out and said, "To keep my man satisfied," and smiled up at him as she locked her lips and tongue around his dick and gave him the best head of his life.

Fifty and Summer fucked like porno stars for two and half hours straight, then jumped into the Jacuzzi as they sipped on some beer and Summer catered to his wounds. "Baby you got to put that ice on it or it's going to stay swollen longer. This will make the swelling go away."

"Damn baby that shit is cold."

"Ice is suppose to be cold!" Summer said, as she looked at Fifty and said, "Honey, can I ask you a personal question?"

"Sure baby, what's up?"

"Well in the club, before the fight broke out, that man called you Fifty! What did he mean by that?"

Fifty laughed and said, "Baby that's my street name!"

"Your name is Fifty?"

Fifty shook his head, yes!

"Are you the same Fifty that's from that Gorilla crew?"

"Yeap, that's me-why have we met before?"

"No, but I heard a lot about you!"

"I hope more good then bad."

"No it wasn't nothin' bad. But, why did you tell me to call you Ice?"

"Because, when I meet people close to where I grow up at, they tend to hear a lot of things about me, and they get a misconception of who I am, or what I'm about, so I chose to use different names to be able to relate to people without them judging me from my past. Do you think that you could have judged me the same if you knew who I was, and the reputation the street has given me?"

"I don't know – I guess if you would've come at me the same way, I couldn't help but love you." Summer said as she caressed his neck.

"Well, I guessed that I judged you wrong, but tell me, does it make a difference now?"

"Hell naw! I'm already sprung on you now! I just better understand the type of man I really got now! And she smiled as she grabbed his dick. "I see that you're ready for round three?"

"You mean round two!" Fifty said as they laughed. "But listen baby, I got a desire that I want to fulfill!'

"Mmmmm! Is that right? What is it?"

"I want to hit that big pretty butt of yours."

"I think that I'll like that!"

"Good, let's get back into the bed; I'll grab the lubricant and rubbers." Fifty said as he got out of the Jacuzzi on rock hard, just thinking about hitting Summer's big fat pretty butt had him hard as steal.

Chapter 8
More Money, More Problems

The next morning Fifty took Summer to I-Hop and they enjoyed a delicious pancake breakfast. Then he gave her a couple of hundred dollars and dropped her off at the motel room, and told her that he'll get back at her later. She enjoyed being with him but knew that he was a hustler and that she had to play her part in order to prove to him that she was down for him and his cause. And now that she knew who he really was, she knew that she had a down and real man, as well as a true gangsta' by her-side, and this made her want him more. Because his reputation alone was big in the streets, and to be known as his lady meant a lot for any woman, so she knew that she had to keep her game tight, because a lot of bitches would be trying to take her position. Summer thought as she soaked in the hot bubble bath with the Victoria Secret apricot scent, and said, "It's us against the world Fifty!" And smiled to herself.

Fifty went to his apartment and took a hot shower then he put on some platinum Sean John jeans, some fresh dark blue suede Timberland's, and a blue stripped Sean John shirt and he wore his black face platinum Rolex watch diamond chain and bracelet, his fat 4 carat diamond ring and his one carat diamond ear rings. Then he looked at his self in the mirror and smiled as he threw on his new blue fitted New York baseball cap, and put his 45 automatic in his waste band. Fifty said to him-self, "Now that's a fly nigga" and smiled at his reflection in the mirror as he picked up his Gucci sports bag and walked out of his apartment.

Fifty went to the bank and grabbed five separate thousand dollar cashier checks and opened up a business account for his Escort Service and put 5g's in it, then went to the post office and mailed them off to Yayo, Power,

Black, Little Chucky and Big Caesar with a card that said, "From blood to the grave, brothers for life. Half a dollar! Loyalty meant everything to Fifty, and he wanted to make sure that his comrades knew that he had their backs and his promise wasn't in vain. Fifty knew all to well that too many niggas act like they're down with other niggas in the pen, but when they get out; they leave nothing but a broken promises behind. Real nigga's do real things and Fake niggas always get exposed.

Fifty pulled up to his next destination, and a young 12 year old boy that he had seen in a picture, was playing with his basketball on the walk-way entrance to his house. It was an old run down two bedroom house, and when the boy saw Fifty walk-up, he stopped bouncing the ball and looked up at him and Fifty said, "Salamu ungo udugu!" And smiled as the young boy's eyes got big. The young kid was well conversed in the Kiswaaki language, but didn't hear no one other then his father, little sister and mother speak it. He knew what Fifty had just said, "Greetings my brother," in Kiswaaki, and he was shocked to hear it from someone else's mouth.

"Is your mother home?" Fifty asked.

"Yes, she's in the house, I'll go get her!"

The boy said as he ran into the house and came back with his mother and 8 year old sister following behind.

Fifty said, "Hello Cleopatra!" He called the big bone, pretty dark brown skin sista, by the nick name that her husband called her. She smiled as Fifty introduced his self, "My name is Fifty, and I'm a very close associate of your husband Big Caesar."

"Oh yeah Fifty, my husband talks very highly of you, it's a pleasure to meet you. Please come in!"

"I apologize but I have to decline, I'm really in a hurry. I just wanted to bring you this and Fifty handed her an envelope with $2,500 dollars in it. Then he said, "You're a blessing to the game, the way you keep it real and ride for your man. I wish that there were more ladies like you! Your man sends his unconditional love to you; here!" And Fifty gave Cleopatra, a jewelry box that had one of the 3 carat lady diamond rings in it.

She opened it and her eyes showed her excitement, as Fifty said," That's from Big Caesar; he wanted to let you know that he loves you! Here's my number, call me if you need anything, and I just sent Big Caesar some money, so he's cool! Bye, Bye Cleo!" Fifty said as he turned and was about to walk away.

"Wait," Cleo said as she hugged Fifty and said, "thank you so much, we needed this so bad,' and kissed him on the cheek as tears rolled down her pretty face.

"Yo ma, you know that the game lord always blesses the real. So don't worry, your realness is felt by the game lord, that why he sent his servant to bless you!"

Cleo said, "You talk just like Big Caesar!" And Fifty smiled as he walked away.

Fifty went by his grandmother's house and gave her $10,000 dollars for her and grandpa to go and ball with, and gave her an additional $20,000 dollars for her to put up for him, incase of an emergency.

He also gave her his attorney business card and private number and a copy of the receipt that the attorney gave him for the retainer's fee. Then he gave his grandmother the other beautiful 3 ½ carat diamond ring and the other 3 ½ carat man's ring for his grandpa.

His grandpa was gone, so grandma put it up for him as she admired her beautiful gift.

Fifty was glad that she loved it, and promised to stop by and let her cook him a home cooked meal soon. Fifty kissed her on the cheek and left. Grandma was kind of upset that he couldn't stay longer, but she knew that the streets had him, and just like a man on a mission, the streets is the only obsession that feeds the desire to his profit and gain.

Fifty pulled up into the Guy Brewer Projects and seen three of his four comrades in the cut getting their serve on. Fifty jumped out of the Range Rover and walked up as Little G-nut said, "Yo Sun, the diamonds is blinding me, look at you, you're doing the most Sun."

"Yeah you look like one of those Rap Stars" Ra added.

"Now that's the way I'm trying to get down Sun!" Juice said as he admired Fifty's diamond pieces.

"How's business?" Fifty asked.

"Yo sun, this muthafuckas jumpin! It's like all the smokers is coming to buy from us now!" Ra said.

"Yeah Sun, they're loving this shit. I sold five ounces already and it ain't even been 24 hours since you gave us the sack. I ain't never sold this much dope this quick before." Little G-Nut said with a big proud grin on his face.

You ain't lying about that, I sold like five and a half ounces too, and it seem like smokers I ain't seen in a long while is poppin back up to buy from me. They said that this is the best shit around, I guess that these smoker got some sort of fuckin internet connection or website chat line, because they're coming way from other projects and areas to buy from us. There goes one of my customers right there – hold up let me get this money." Juice said as he ran over to serve a smoker.

Fifty laughed as he seen his little comrades all run and go serve some customers of theirs. And Fifty walked back over to his truck to grab the pint of Hennessy and cups, that he stop and got at the liquor store before he came to the projects. He wanted to kick it with his little comrades for a minute, so he could better feel them out.

Fifty looked up and seen a Red Vett pass by slowly looking-hard, Fifty instantly recognized the nigga who was driving as the nigga name Red from the Bus Station, who that stripper bitch Tee-Tee was transporting for. Red had another big black bald headed dude with him sitting on the passenger side as they passed by.

Then an old brown 78 Cadillac Fleetwood hit the corner, and came to a fast stop in front of the projects, as three masked niggas jumped out of a Cadillac blasting.

Fifty dropped the bag with the Hennessy in it, and pulled his gun out as he seen the first nigga shoot at Ra, but the bullets hit the base head that Ra was serving in the back.

Ra ducked behind a car as Fifty shot four shots from his big black 45 automatic, and two of the hollo point bullets caught one of the mask man in the upper part of his body as he fell to the ground holding his chest.

The second mask man saw his buddy fall, and turned his attention from Little G-nut to Fifty, and busted two shots from his 12 gage knocking out the window from the car that Fifty was duckin' behind. Little G-nut jumped from behind a tree, with two gloc' 9mm in his hand bustin like crazy, he hit the second nigga with the 12 gage, 4 times and dropped him to the concrete, as he empty the other shots in the drivers side car door, leaving the door riddled with bullet holes.

The third masked man came up with a Mac-11 shooting wildly. A bullet hit Juice in the arm as he traded shots with the third mask man. Juice had a big chrome 357 magnum and was knocking big holes in the car that was around the third man. Ra started bustin at the third man too when he saw Juice get hit. Fifty ran across the parking lot and grabbed two little girls that was playing hop scotch across the street, and threw them behind a park car as the man on the driver seat of the Cadillac reached out of the window bustin his 9mm in every direction.

Fifty got hit in the shoulder while he was saving the little girls, but he came back up bustin, emptying his 45 automatic in the back of the Cadillac window. The man with the Mac-11 snatched up one of the mask man, and jumped in the back seat of the car, and the other one stood-up bustin wildly, as he ran around the car and jumped into the passenger side of the car right as Baby Tank came running out of the building, in his boxer's shorts and Timberland boots and firing his AR-15 rifle at the Cadillac. The Cadillac punched out, as Baby Tank ran into the street and started bustin at the back of the car like Rambo, the trunk to the car flew-up and the Cadillac swerved and hit a parked car before regaining control and turned the corner.

"Are ya'll alright?" Baby Tank asked as he looked around at his comrades.

"Yeah, we cool." Fifty said, as he wiped his blood off one of the little girls face.

The little girl's mother came running outside shouting "My babies, my babies – Tiffany, Tasha are you O'kay? OH…. Shit! Tiffany you bleeding!"

"She's alright, that's my blood on her," said Fifty. The mother saw Fifty was bleeding from his shoulder and was relieved that it wasn't her baby-girls.

"Thank you for saving my babies that was a very brave thing you did, and I'm so grateful."

"The lord won't forgive me if I let one of his little pretty angels get shot." Fifty said as he smiled and pinched one of the little girl fat cheeks, then him and Baby Tank walked over to check on Ra, Juice and Little G-nut. Little G-nut and Ra was standing around Juice looking at his gun-shot wound.

"Is he alright?" Fifty asked.

"Yeah, he's cool, he just got hit in the arm, we're going to take him to Mrs. Annie Mae in apartment 125, she's a retired nurse. She'll hook him up for us, you need to come too!" Ra said as he saw the blood running down Fifty's arm.

"What about him?" Fifty gestured toward the base head that was holding his upper chest.

"I'm cool ya'll, it just went in and out of me. Just let me get something fat for this 20 dollars and I'll be on my way."

"Listen, come with us so you can get hooked up, and I'll hook you up with something fat before you leave."

"O'kay." The base head said; he was happy that the gangsters didn't dog him out and leave him for dead.

"Little G-nut!" Fifty said as he looked over at his little comrade. "Get some smokers to pick up these bullet shells, and have them wash down the blood stains, give who-ever helps you a fat 20 dollar rock."

"Yo Sun, I'm on it!" Little G-nut said as he walked away.

"Go put on some clothes and help Little G-nut clean his shit up." Fifty told Baby Tank. "Ra, watch their backs and keep the customers happy."

"I got you!"

"Juice!"

"What's up Rade?"

"Lead the way!" Fifty said as he and the smoker followed Juice to Ms. Annie Mae's apartment, where she went to work, sewing them up.

Since the smokers' wound was the worse, Fifty let him go first, and the base head was pleased to be given that kind of respect. Fifty took Juice sack, and gave the base head 8 fat $20 dollar rocks, and said, "Keep your money, that's for taking one for the home team. Now keep this incident a secret, because we don't respect snitches around here, and running around telling people what happened here today, is like snitching on us. Someone might tell the police about it and it might result in some consequences, so keep your damn mouth shut. You dig?"

"Yo Sun, I respect ya! You guy's keep it one hundred percent Sun! You ain't got to worry about me running my mouth – its respect Sun!"

"Good, now let the people who want to buy the good shit, know where to come."

"You got that Sun – I'm out, peace kid!"

The base head said as he rushed out to go enjoy his come up.

Mrs. Annie Mae finish sewing Juice up and Fifty said, "So what we owe you Ma?"

"Whatever you can stand to give me – I'm good baby," Mrs. Annie Mae said with a loving smile.

Fifty pulled out his bank roll and peeled off a thousand dollars and gave it to her.

"Oh baby, this is way too much, I can't take all that!"

"I can never pay you enough for the loyalty and devotion that you gave to me and my comrades. We appreciate you Ma!" And Fifty gave her a kiss on the cheek, as Juice did the same, and they walked out.

One thing about the projects, the police don't give a damn about whether a nigga live or die's, and people don't care to call the police much either, they deal with their own issues the best way that they know how. Fifty seen a small crowd around Ra, and went to see what the problem was, "What's up Rade?"

"Man these people is light weight beefin about their shit getting shot up. Them two muthafucka's cars got windows shot out. This old smoked out bitch here is talking about her window to her apartment got shot out. I know for a fact that, that shit was already broken, and that old man, got bullet holes the size of golf balls in his new Buick."

"O'kay, give the woman who got the broken window to her apartment a fat $20 dollar rock. And tell the rest of them to come and speak to me.

"O'kay word!" Ra said as he left and sent the other three people over to him.

"O'kay, who's car window got shot out? You two? O'kay, here!" Fifty gave them $600 dollars a piece.

"I think it cost a little more then this!" One of the men said.

"Fool, you better go to the junk yard and buy you a window for $30 dollars, and take it down to Jake's glass and have him put it in for twenty.

"Oh, I didn't think of that!"

"Well nigga, you better start thinking!" Fifty said as the two people walked away.

"Damn old timer, look like they tried to kill your car!"

"That's what I said! Muthafuckas need to learn how to shoot. And I seen the way you ran over there and grabbed them two little girls, and moved them out of the way of the gun fire that was a brave and good thing you did!"

"Well, if it's time for me to die, then let me die, but don't kill an innocent soul because then I'll have to suffer in life." Fifty said as he looked the old man deep in his eyes.

"I respect that son!" The old man said.

"So let me see, here! I hope that this can help you get your ride back looking new again." Fifty then handed him a thousand dollars.

"I'm sure it will...! Thank you son and ya'll be careful out there!"

"We will....!" Fifty said as he turned and walked away. He went over to where his comrades was standing in the cut and heard Little G-nut say, "Man I just jumped from behind the tree with both guns in hand, and got to bustin! I fuckin put a lease six in his chest!"

"Yeah, you fucked him up Rade!" Ra said laughing'!

"Yo, I just heard gun shots – I was fuckin fat Ka-Ka big butt ass from the back, and it sound like all hell broke loose, so I pulled my dick out and threw my boxers on – you know! I keep the Tims on anyway for traction, so I ran and grabbed the AR-15 and run out ready to get it crackin Sun! I was mad when I seen them fools pulling off, I wanted to blow one of them bitches backs out! Yo, my word Sun!" Baby Tank said as he expressed the depth of his emotions with his body language.

"Yo Fifty, you saved my ass! That fool would've probably killed me if you didn't get at him when you did. Yo Sun, that's love!" Ra said as he gave Fifty a ghetto embrace.

"Yo that's the way we get down Sun! We're family. We got to watch each-other backs. But what I tell you guys?

I know that them niggas was going to try to make a move on us, we're taking food out of a niggas mouth! Now it's about who's going to be the king of the jungle!"

"Yo, do you think that Red sent them niggas?" Juice asked.

"Yo, your muthafucken right he did! That nigga passed by in a Red Vett right before them niggas hit the corner and jumped out. That ain't no got damn coincidence!" Fifty said.

"Yo Sun, let's go lay them nigga down! Yo, fuck them pussy ass niggas Sun – they can't fuck with the gorillas." Ra said in a hyped voice. "Yeah Fifty, what's up Sun were riding on them niggas tonight right?" Little G-nut asked with excitement in his voice.

"Naw, tonight won't be good! Those niggas will be expecting us to retaliate on them if we suspect them. So we wait for a few days and catch them while they're sleeping, and we do it right!"

"Yo, just tell us when and how you want to put it down, and it's on! Baby Tank expressed.

"O'kay listen, I want you'll to find two reliable base heads that would stand out front, and direct traffic into the cut over there. That's where I want ya'll to post up, over their and over there! Pay them a 50 rock a piece, and feed them when you eat. I'ma fined out some things that we need to know so we can do it right. Ya'll stay focused, and watch each-others back. If you need me, you got my number."

"Yo alright Sun – we got you!" Juice said as Fifty gave them all their secret hand shake and jumped into his truck and left.

Chapter 9
O'kay, Let's Play

It was later that same night at around 10:30p.m., when Fifty pulled up and parked at the popular strip club called the Attic, and he was dressed to impress with some black silk slacks, black gator boots, and a nice beige Sean John thick turtle neck sweater. Fifty had on his diamond pieces, but they were hidden to the naked eyes. The waitress escorted him to a seat, and he ordered a double shot of Hennessy. The cute dark skin waitress took his order and smiled, then walked away switching her big sexy fat ass! Fifty look around and seen that the place was packed, and the women was all thick to death and running around half naked with ass and tit's dancing all over the place. Fifty knew exactly what was on the person's mind who created the G-string panties and thongs.

A pretty sista walked over to Fifty looking Puerto Rican and Black, wearing a sexy red G-string bathing suit that complimented her beautiful gold complexion and nice fat titties to the max. "Would you like a lap dance Poppy?" The sista' said in her sexiest tone.

Fifty looked up at her and said, "Baby if I had a trace of sucka characteristic in me, then believe me – you will surely exposed it"! But unfortunately, trickin is against my religion – and I think that we're in the same profession, because we both desire to play and trim suckas, tricks, and Vic's."

Then they both smiled realizing that they both were motivated by the same impulse. Fifty continued, "But you just use a different kind of approach and weapon then me." (He moved his sleeve to his sweater up briefly to act like he was looking at the time and to let her get a glimpse of his new Povade Presidential Rolex watch) "And I must admit; the lord has taken pride in dressing you up with beauty." He smiled as she nonchalantly struck a sexy pose and blushed.

"So what kind of approach do you use?" She said as she slid in the booth next to him. The waitress brought Fifty his drink and Fifty said, "Can you bring my friend here whatever she like's to drink too!" Then Fifty peeled off a hundred dollar bill and gave it to the waitress and said, "Keep the change!"

"Thank you sir, - what would you like Nina?"

"Oh I'll have my regular!"

"Apple juice and Absolute right?"

"Yes..!"

"O'kay, I'll be right back with it!" The waitress said as she walked off.

"Well baby, my approach is simple, I just keep it real. I tend to meet beautiful women like yourself, who desire something more out of life, and who's tired of these sucka's doggin' them, disrespecting them, and using them as ten dollar hoes, and then kicking them to the curve when they're tired of them." (Fifty knew that he had to assassinate these niggas character, and make her feel used and abused so she would despise every sucka in the club,) Fifty took a sip of his Hennessy and let his words irritate her thoughts for a second; then he said, "I just hate to see these sucka-dogs take advantage of real and down sista's. You ladies deserve to be respected and treated like ladies, regardless of your profession or how you choose to get your money. So what, a woman chooses to trade an exotic fantasy for money, that don't take away from her substance." Fifty said as the waitress set Nina's drink on the table.

"If you need anything else just wave."

"O'kay thank you beautiful!" Fifty said, as the waitress smiled and walked away with a little more sway in her hips.

Fifty looked back at Nina and said, "So I just help a women establish better security in her life by helping her to receive what she rightfully deserves. These sucka's tend to use beautiful women like yourself, and when they finish with them, the women don't have nothing but a couple of new out-fits and some worthless jewelry.

Therefore, I tell my ladies to put their money up and invest it in a business and real-estate. Do you rather have a sucka give you a couple of thousand here and there to lease that pussy, or would you rather have 50 to 100 thousand dollars in one woop, that you can put aside, and after you kick his pathetic ass to the curve, then you can do something beneficial for yourself."

"I rather have 50 to 100 thousand and do me!" Nina said with a girlish giggle.

"Of course, because how many niggas who you cater to will give you 50 to 100 thousand dollars to start you a business if you asked them?"

"None!"

"You damn right, cause these sucka's want to keep you broke and doing bad, so they can always be able to take advantage of you."

"You ain't lying either, I had a couple of niggas dog me out like that! I thought that I was his ride or die bitch and all, but come to find out; he had two other bitches with his kids. When I found out about it, he kicked me to the curve, and said that I was just his side kick."

"I feel you Shorty, and one thing about them kind of dumb ass nigga, they always expose their hand to the side kick.

They show them where the stash spots is, or the hide away house, or she might even stumble across his main house where him and his baby momma stay, and he keeps all of his stash there.

A lot of baby momma's learn about the side kick and set up the move, because they rather have a bulk of money put up to the side so if he chooses to run off with the side kick, then she will still be secure.

Bitches ain't dumb no more, they rather have security for themselves, instead of broken promises, and stuck with a broken heart. And like I said, I believe in keeping it real, I give my companions half of the money that I get, but I keep all of the other stuff."

"Shoot that ain't bad! I know a couple of niggas that we can get, and I got the entire scoop on them!"

"Well baby, I think that fate must've brought us together!" Fifty said as they both smiled. "Listen baby, we got to get together soon and explore our options and feel each-other out."

"I get off work at 2:00a.m., if you want to come and get me after work, then we can go kick it then, and get better acquainted."

"That sounds very promising!"

"You know what's crazy?" She said.

"No what?"

"I don't even know your name!"

After Nina said that they were interrupted by Tee-Tee as she walked up wearing a dark burgundy G-string and a wife beater T-shirt that was tide up in the front, with some dark burgundy suede high heel pumps, and she was killin' the game looking thick in all the right places.

"Hey Fifty, what's up baby! I was thinking of you, how you been doing?" Tee-Tee said as she lend over and gave him a big kiss.

"I'm doing good Ma, and yourself?"

"I'm doing fine, thanks to you!" She said with a big smile.

Nina looked at Fifty and then at Tee-Tee.

"Hi Nina!" Tee-Tee said.

"Hi Tee-Tee!"

"Listen baby, why don't you go and write that information down for me, and give me a minute with Tee-Tee!"

"O'kay Poppy." Nina said as she slid out the booth and walked away with a sexy switch in her hips. With a nice J. Lo ass on her, but Tee-Tee had an ass like Lisa Raye and knew how to show it off.

"Wow, it's good to see you, I must've thought about you every day since that day we met!"

"Well that's good to know, and it's good to see you too Ma! Damn, what's that?"

"Oh nothing!"

"Damn Ma, you hiding bruises now with make-up, what's up with that?"

"Well you probably guessed, after the police let us go at the bus station...... thank God! He took me to his spot and started trippin and shit, and kicked my ass!" Tee-Tee said as a tear rolled down her cheek and she stared down at the table in a daze.

"Yo Ma – talk to me, you know that you're fuckin with the real.....you know my style!"

She looked up at Fifty and said, "and then he told me that I had to pay him back his 80g's one way or another, and pulled his gun on me and said that I was going to have to sell pussy for him until I pay him back every penny, and made me (and she paused) made me fuck his whole crew and told me that I still owed him 79 thousand. So now he set me up with his partners, and made me have sex with them to pay him back." And tears were rolling down her cheek!

"Yo Ma, wipe your tears baby – it's going to be alright. I got your back Ma, haven't I always had your back?" She looked at him and shook her head, yes.

"Well, it was a reason for you to come into my life, because the game Lord sent me to watch over you." She looked at him and smiled! "Yo listen Ma, do you know where this bitch ass nigga lives?"

"Yeah, he took me to his house one time, he got a big house on twenty-second street."

"Do you know how to get there?"

"Yes…!"

"What time can you get off?"

"Now if I want!"

"Well go get dressed, we got business to handle!" Tee-Tee smiled excitedly and got up and rushed to get dressed as Nina came back with her name and number on a piece of paper.

"Here Poppy!"

"Yo Ma, peep! I'ma come and get you tomorrow and take you out to lunch, so we can spend sometime and check our traps together. I wish I could've kicked it with you tonight, but something came up, and I always take care of my girls first and foremost. So when you get with me, then you know that I'll also put you first, even before other beautiful half naked woman's with killer bodies." Fifty said, with a smile as he ran his finger down her hip and she started blushing.

"I understand baby – I'll be waiting for your call tomorrow." Nina said, as she rubbed her fingers down his waves and gave him a seductive smile then walked away.

Fifty said, "Checkmate!"

Ten minutes later Tee-Tee walked out in some tight white Guess jeans, and a red Polo button down shirt that was tide at the bottom to show off her stomach, and some red suede stiletto boots, looking as fine and sexy as a video model. She walked up and grabbed Fifty's hand as they walked out. Nina was looking at them from a distance, and loved the way that Fifty grabbed Tee-Tee's hand and walked out, because it showed that he had respect for his ladies, even if they did strip and hustled with some tricks on the side.

Nina was excited about being down with Fifty, because she heard a lot of good things about him, and she knew that he was a down and real nigga through his street reputation. She smiled as she turned her butt around and wiggled it in this fat ugly nigga's crotch, and he put another $10 dollar bill in her g-string.

* * * *

Fifty hit his alarm to his new range Rover truck and Tee- Tee smiled and said, "damn, I'm scared of you," Fifty smiled as he opened up the passenger side door for her, and then closed it and went around and jumped into the driver seat as Tee-Tee said, "I see that it don't take you long at all!"

"You know what they say baby, real niggas do real things," and Fifty smiled as he pulled off.

Tee-Tee took Fifty and showed him where Red's main house was at, and Fifty seen the Red Vett parked in the drive-way. Fifty wrote down the address, and then they drove back toward the Guy Brewer Projects, and Tee-Tee showed Fifty where a couple of Red's crew member lived, and pointed to the house where they all kick it at.

Fifty passed by and seen a lot of cars parked in the driveway and on the street as if it was a hang out or something. Tee-Tee said that, that was the house that Red took her to when they raped her.

She said the only good thing about it was, that they all used protection, so she wouldn't have their DNA in her, in case she decided to call the police.

Tee-Tee then showed Fifty where Red's right hand man name Crime lived, he was the big bald headed dude, and Fifty seen a new big blue Ford Excursion truck parked in the drive-way. Tee-Tee said that he's the one who sodomized her, and she wanted to kill him herself.

Fifty seen revenge in her eyes, and knew that she would do anything to get even.

Fifty stopped at the liquor store and grabbed his needed necessities, and went to grab a motel with a Jacuzzi at the Merriot where the room was plushed and expensive, and he knew that not to many niggas would be going their, trying to fuck off that much cash on a piece of ass and a one night stand. Also it made a bitch feel important, and not like a ten dollar hoe.

When they walked in the room Tee-Tee said "Oooowow a Jacuzzi, I need a nice hot bubble message, and started washing the Jacuzzi down and filling it up. Fifty thought to himself, "Damn that was easy – who's chasing who?" Then he saw Tee-Tee strip down to her g-string and wife beater t-shirt. Fifty said, "I guess that answered that question" as he pour them both a cup of Absolute and Cranapple juice on ice. Tee-Tee walked up and hugged Fifty and said, "If you want, I'll go with you, because I want to put some closure to my conscious too, knowing that I didn't let a nigga get away with doggin' me like that."

"I feel you Ma, and I'll see what I can do, but I got to make the best decision that won't get us caught up, and I got to know and be sure that I can trust you and that your down for me like I'm down for you."

"I will be baby, I promise! You've been the only man in my life that has been down with me from the start, and you saved my life whether you believe so or not. And for that, I'm totally grateful, and I want to be down for you in the same way."

"I feel you Shorty," Fifty said as he went over and cut the water off on the Jacuzzi and cut on the radio to slow grooves as Keith Sweat and Cut Close old song Twisted was playing.

"But I don't know if I could fully accept you in my life? The only woman that I will except are women who are down with me on getting money for this Escort Service that I'm about to put down. I got one down bottom bitch on my team that I know is real and about me, but I know that one bottom bitch is never good enough to satisfy a player of my caliber, so I'm looking for another down and real lady, who I can embrace in my life as my other bottom lady and soulmate.

I think that I might have someone who qualifies, but I don't know if she's strong enough to handle the position of a bottom lady. Beauty is only good for pageants and strip clubs, I need brains, strength, and thoroughness to go with it."

Tee-Tee instantly thought that Fifty was talking about Nina, and knew that she would make a better bottom lady then Nina. Tee-Tee walked up and sat on Fifty's lap and said, "Baby I could be down for you like that… and I'm down and thorough."

Fifty knew that Tee-Tee was a thorough bitch, because she didn't call the police on Red's sorry ass for doing that foul and disrespectful shit to her.

Fifty also knew that he had to make sure that she had hoe qualities, and not just turned out on some forceful shit. Fifty said, "listen baby, I know what that bitch ass nigga did to you was some horrible and disrespectful shit, and for him to continue to force you to sell your body for his profit and gain, is even more disrespectful, and I don't believe in taking advantage of a woman like that.

If a woman is already devoted to that profession, then I respect it and will except her as my companion, because as a true hustler, I do respect all kinds of hustle, and I feel that if a woman's down enough for me to hustle and trick with her body, so we can prosper together, as a real nigga, I'ma make sure that her needs is met, and she has the best that we can afford. Therefore, I will not accept a woman who's not already devoted to that aspect of the game."

Tee-Tee looked at Fifty and knew that she had to come clean or she would lose out on the chance to become apart of his life. So she said, "Baby I didn't say that I never turn a trick before. I did many times for money, that's how I first met Red, he tricked with me, then asked me if I wanted to make some extra money, that's how I first started bringing dope back for him. I just don't respect the way he did me, and the way he's forcing me to turn tricks with his friends and clients, or threaten to kill me if I don't. Like I said, I don't mind turning tricks for my man, but let me choose my man, and I want to chose you, that is, if you will accept me!"

Fifty looked at her and said, "Shorty, in order to become one of my bottom ladies, you have to be able to respect my word as law, and never let nothing or no one come between your loyalty and devotion to me, and our cause. You'll have a sister in your life that will be your equal, and you must keep her game in check, just like she'll do you.

Together you both will have the duty to build us a strong, and down, and devoted stable of beautiful women who know how to hustle, so we all can get paid and have the best, and jealousy can never poison your heart and mind, because as my bottom lady you must know that you are a reflection of me until the end.

Other women may come and go, but you and my lady Summer I believe would always withstand the test of time. Do you think that you can abide by these rules and obligations?"

"Yes, "Tee-Tee said with a big smile.

"Well you must know the first rule of devotion in my life, and live by it!"

"What's that?"

"Always keep your man satisfied." Tee-Tee smiled and said, "I like that rule....... What's number two?

"Get the money!" And they both started laughing as Tee-Tee started passionately kissing Fifty, and when she relaxed in his arms, he let out a painful moan. And she lend back up and said, "Baby what's wrong?"

"Oh nothing, I got shot today and my shoulder's a little sore."

"You got shot! Where at? Damn, baby what happened?"

"Me and my man had to get at some Puerto Rican dudes from the Bronx, and I got hit during the shoot out."

"Your wild! Come on let's get in the Jacuzzi so we can practice on rule number one!" Tee-Tee said, as she started undressing him. Fifty got naked and grabbed his rubber and put one on, as he watched Tee-Tee bend over the Jacuzzi fixing the water temperature and her ass was looking lovely. Tee-Tee and Summer was a perfect match, Fifty thought as he walked over to the Jacuzzi and slid his dick right into Tee- Tee's hot wet, tight pussy, and begin to satisfy his long awaited desires, as he said to himself, "Checkmate!

Chapter 10
Ball in'

It was the following morning and Fifty was back at his town house cooking up a couple of more keys. Little G-nut called early in the morning at 8:15a.m. and told Fifty that they all was on their last ounces, and it was going quick.

Fifty laughed, and told him that he'll catch up with them in a couple of hours. Fifty finished cooking the last half of bird, and started weighting it out in ounces, and putting the ounces in separate plastic baggies.

He smiled at the way he put his game down on Tee-Tee making her think that he was going to smash Red for her, when he planned on doing it anyway, and just needed the right information to be able to do it right, and profit at the same time.

Now Fifty could put the jack move down too, and smash this whole crew at the same time. And on top of that, he knocked one of the baddest hoes in the game, making him have two of the downest bitches in the game, and he knew that them two beautiful bitches alone is a million dollar come up, and if he knocks that bad ass Puerto Rican and black bitch Nina, then he'll kill the game, because just them three hoes can walk into any stripper contest and win by a land slid.

Fifty knew that he had to play on these bitches right, because one false move would get a nigga fucked up for life!

Fifty pondered the thought, and then smiled at his devilish idea, and said to himself, "Checkmate."

Fifty went and picked up his grandfather and had his grandfather rent him a nice black 1999 Cadillac Seville.

They caravanned to Fifty's new town house and Fifty's grandpa was proud to see Fifty doing good. Fifty gave his grandpa his extra key in case of an emergency, and the combination to the safe.

Grandpa was glad that Fifty trusted him like this, and they felt a special bond as Fifty dropped him back off. He waved at his grandma and rushed back to pick up the dope for his crew, and headed for the projects.

Fifty knew that it would be like playing Russian Roulette if he tried to deliver the dope to his crew in his fixed up Range Rover, so he grabbed the rental so he could get around without all of the unnecessary attention.

He pulled in the project parking lot and got out of the rental car with the factory tint, and Little G-nut was close by behind a parked car and said, " Damn Sun, you was on death row kid! I didn't know who you was, I thought you was another nigga trying to pull a creep move Sun!"

Fifty laughed as they started walking toward Little G-nut and their apartment.

"Fifty said, "Yo Sun, you can't be running up on any and everybody that you don't know as they pull up into these projects, other people live here too, and they got family, friends, and even other people like social workers and shit. So you got to be more inconspicuous with your acts and actions. Or you guys is going to shoot an innocent person and fuck off your whole game. Feel Me?"

"Yeah Sun, I feel you, but them sucka got us up on pins and needles around here. When are we going to ride on them fools Sun?"

"Soon Rade - real soon!" They walked into the apartment, and the rest of the crew was sitting on the couch smoking weed and playing Sega Genesis as they patiently waited for Fifty to arrive.

"Yo Sun, what's up Rade!'" Baby Tank said, as he paused the game and they all got up and gave Fifty their secret hand shake. Then they all handed him Nine Thousand Dollars a piece with a big smile.

"I see ya'll niggas in here slippin playing this damn game." Fifty scolded.

"Never Sun, that's why we had Little G-nut posted outside! Ra said, with a big smile.

"You can sleep on this game if you want to, we ain't the only beast in the jungle….. believe that!" Fifty said as he opened up the black bag and handed everyone another 18 ounces a piece. "Now listen Rades, I got a trace on the nigga Red's main spot and also his right hand mans house, as well as their playhouse where all them niggas hang out at. So be ready to move in a couple of days. I need to secure some shit before we push this line, because if we fuck up, then we all will be eating our next month meals in the prison chow hall. But if everything get put down right, then we all should come off with a nice little extra cash in our pockets."

"That's what I'm talking about Sun!" Ra stated.

"O'kay listen, I've put together some moves that I need ya'll to put down for me, and you got to do it exactly as I say. Now Ra, I need you to find one of your reliable base head and take him to buy both of these cars out of the auto trade that I highlighted. Have him tell the owner that he's waiting for his driver license to come back from the DMV, but he needs transportation now, because he just started a new job and needs to get back and forth to work. Nine time out of ten, the owner will say fuck it and sell the car, because they obviously need the money. So tell him to use an alias name to purchase the car with, and bring them here, and make sure that you wipe it down and use gloves when you fuck with it, because we don't need no finger prints left on it. You dig?"

"Hell yeah Sun, that's some vicious game too, because the cars won't be on the police hot sheet, and we won't have to worry about getting pulled over on a fluke."

"Exactly!" Fifty said.

"O'kay! Here's $2,500 hundred dollars for the cars and give the base head this for looking out for us." And Fifty gave Ra a fat hundred dollar rock.

"Now Juice, I need you to call your man that you was telling me had the guns for sale, and grab us some proper shit, I want six of those new Gloc's and see if he got something to keep them quiet! Cause we don't want to wake the neighbors, if you know what I mean?" Fifty and his crew laughed as Fifty handed Juice $3,500 hundred dollars. "Here that should cover it."

"Got you!" Juice said, as he grabbed the stack of hundred dollar bills.

"Yo Sun, whatcha need us to do?" Little G-nut asked.

"Here, grab the stuff on this list for us and I need you to also hold down the spot and get money. It looks like your clientele has picked up big, and it's around 8 base heads out-side right now looking for ya'll. So do your thang and I'll be at ya'll soon. So stay posted and watch your backs, G-day is around the corner." Fifty said, as everyone smiled. And he gave them all their secret hand shake and said "Meeting adjourn" and walked out!

Fifty rolled up to his attorney's office and grabbed the documents to his new escort business, then rolled down to the out skirts of the Jamaica Estates area where he had a 2:00 o'clock appointment with one of his attorney's Mr. Kutler, attorney friends, who had possession of a beautiful baby mansion that he wanted to lease out for one of his clients who relocated one of his businesses to Italy, and is now living out there so he could get his business up and running appropriately.

The lease was only for one year, but that was fine by Fifty. It was a beautiful seven bedrooms and six and a half bathrooms baby mansion sitting on one and a quarter acres of land. It had marble floors and counter tops, two fire places, a Jacuzzi bath and a see through shower in the master bedroom, a living room, family room, den and a big state of the art home theater room. It also had a five car garage, a big nine foot pool with a Jacuzzi and basketball and tennis court. It was worth 2.3 million, but the attorney was allowing the lease to go for $6,000 thousand dollars a month.

Fifty fell in love with the baby mansion as soon as he walked inside, it was a hustler dream, and he had to have it.

"So Mr. Grant how much is it for the total move in cost?" Fifty asked trying to hide his excitement.

"Well Fifty, since you're a good friend of Kutler, I'll give it to you for 12 thousand down. That's your first, last, and security deposit. And since Mr. Kutler vaguely explained your position, I'll be glad to put it under your escort business name, to exclude you from any possible red flags. I do understand a hustler perspective. But if you by any chance should take a fall, and your payments stop, then I would repossess the property and release it to the next interested party in line. Deal?"

"Deal!" Fifty uttered as he said "would you take cash?"

"I don't see why not!" Mr. Grant said as they shook hands and closed the deal.

Fifty had the lease to his new baby mansion and knew that it was time to take the game to a whole nother level. He smiled full of excitement as he pulled up to the Q Motel Inn, and saw his superstar at work as she walked a old white man back to his car and wave him bye! She had on a sexy black mini dress out-fit that wasn't hiding nothin'. Fifty stepped out of the Seville and Summer's eyes lite up with joy as she seen him.

"Daddy," she said as she rushed over to his side and gave him a smile.

"How's my leading lady doing!" Fifty asked as she approached him.

"I'm doing fine now that you're here, but come on inside so I can wash up. You know that I'll never embrace you after I been with a trick."

"That's respect!" Fifty said as he followed Summer in her other room.

"I'll be back in ten minutes, let me jump in the shower and get cleaned up for you." Summer said as she pulled her one piece mini skirt out-fit over her head, and switched her sexy thick naked ass to the bathroom.

Fifty watched her fat ass switch seductively to the bathroom, and said, "Witchcraft!" And smiled as he cut on the radio and started reciting the lyrics to Snoop Dogg's new cut.

Summer came out of the bathroom 15 minutes later butt naked, baby oiled up, and smelling like Victoria Secret peach. She walked up to Fifty and gave him a big seductive kiss and Fifty squeezed her big sexy ass as he said, "Damn Ma, you smell good".

"You do to daddy!" She said, as she squeezed his dick through his nice velour Nautica sweat paints and said, "I missed you," as his dick instantly got hard.

He knew at this point he couldn't resist, so he said, "well why don't you show me how much!"

And she giggled as she started undressing him. She seen the white medical patch on his shoulder and said "Ooowow baby, what happened?"

"Oh it's nothing, I had a shoot out and got shot, that's all!" Fifty said as he finished getting undressed.

"That's all", Summer said, as she looked at him for some sort of explanation, and when she didn't receive one, she just shook her head and laughed and said, "you're crazy."

"I know, I've been told that a lot." Fifty joked as he put back on his light blue Tims.

"What are you doing?" Summer asked.

"I'ma need the traction, because I'm about to put in some work!" Fifty said as he gave her a devilish grin, and pulled her to him as they passionately kissed and embraced and Fifty picked her up and sat her back against the wall, and they were fuckin' like porno stars. Fifty made her touch everything in the motel room, and then bent her legs all the way back and pounded his way to ecstasy.

When they finished, it was 6:00 o'clock that evening, and Fifty took her to eat at a local Mexican restaurant and put her up on game.

He said, "Yo ma, I got some jewels that I want to lay down on you, that I've been working on to better our struggles and place you in a better position in this game.

Now peep Ma, I respect all game, but the best game is a secure game, and it's only right that we take this game to the next level, because I know that your sex is priceless, and even though you got the block on lock, I believe that I would not be considered a real nigga if I didn't elevate your game and potentials to a higher level. So I took the liberty of establishing an escort service for us, so you can be the boss bitch that I know you are." (Summer's eyes got big with excitement as her body language showed her approval.)

"But I also know that one down ass bottom lady wouldn't satisfy my desires and ambition, because one's to close to having none! So I accepted another woman in my life that would be equal to you as my bottom lady and your sister in this game. Together you both will build and run this service and make sure our money is right, and the other bitches stay in check. You'll watch her back, and be down for her the same as you would for me, and she'll be down for you the same way. You'll keep her in check when she needs your support, and she will do the same for you.

This is law! Now If you don't think that you could abide by these terms that I'm laying down, then you have the choice to reject it now, and I'll give you your chosen fee back so you can leave".

"No daddy, I'm down with you, if that's what you want, then I'ma respect your desires and wishes. You're my man, and I'm down with you to the fullest. And I'll be down with her the same!"

"Good, I knew that you were 1000% down with me, but I had to make sure." Fifty said with a serious look on his face.

"So when will I meet her?"

"Soon baby, but first I got to work out some fine details and put our game all the way in effect, and I need a favor from you!"

"Sure baby, whatever you need!"

"Can you get me a credit card off one of your tricks tonight, without them knowing?"

"Of course, that's easy! Do you want the ID too?"

"Only if the nigga looks like me!" Fifty said in a joking manner.

"Well that's out the question!" Summer said as she kissed his lips and giggled.

"Yo, but try to catch a sucka who got some paper – because a bullshit credit card might not work."

"I'll see what I can do!"

"Good I got to attend to some business, so let me catch up with you later on tonight."

"O'kay baby," Summer said, as they got up and existed the restaurant..

* * * *

It was 9:30p.m. when Fifty pulled up in front of the old brick run down house with his music bumpin. A second later he seen the object to his scandalous intentions walking out the door, and jumped into the Range Rover as

119

Fifty turned his music down to a mellow tone, as the pleasant sounds of Franky Beverly and Maze echoed thought the speakers.

"Hi Poppy, Nina said as she closed the passenger door."

"Hello my butter pecan Puerto Rican!" Fifty said as Nina lend over and gave him a kiss on the cheek. She was looking as beautiful and sexy as a sex symbol. She had on a bad black leather pants out fit with the leather vest to match, and some black leather stiletto boots with the silver high heels and tips. Fifty knew right away that she spent a lot of her money, as well as her Suga daddy's money on clothes.

"This Range Rover is like that."

"Thank you Ma, you know a nigga got to keep his game tight."

"I see," she said with a seductive smile.

"Do you like sea food?" Fifty asked.

"Yeah – I'm a sea food fanatic!"

"Good, I know this nice sea food restaurant out the way that's off the hook! And it's in a cool area, so we can enjoy some quality time together without niggas being all up in our mix. Feel Me!"

"Yeah! I'm with you tonight, so wherever you want to go, I'm down!"

"Where-ever?" Fifty asked with a seductive grin.

Nina giggled and said, "Yeap, I'm with you tonight Poppy!

"Damn, I love the sound of that! Fifty said as he gave her a player smile, and cut up the music as the CD player changed songs to a 'loose ends old school song,' "You Got Me Hanging On A String" came On.

"Oooowow, that's the cut." Nina said as she started slowly dancing to the beat and softly singing the song.

Fifty glanced over at her and smiled as he got a good look at her fine ass, and estimated that she was only around 19 to 21 years old.

Ten minutes later, Fifty and Nina was at the table of a nice expensive sea food restaurant under a dim candle light, as they sipped some white wine and waited for their order to arrive.

Fifty said, "So give me the 411 on these suckas' that you got in mind?"

"Well, I use to fuck with this nigga name Black Rob out of the 40 projects, and he dogged the shit out of me. But that's another story. Do you know him?"

"Yeah, I heard about him, he suppose to be ballin pretty hard I heard." Fifty played like he didn't really know him personally, but the truth is they were old school enemies from back in the day. Black Rob was hooked up with the Supreme crew, the same crew that Fifty and his comrades smashed in the pen just before he got out. Fifty believed that Black Rob was the one who blew his comrade Money-G head off, after they robbed him. "Ain't he a older black ass nigga who's tall and bald headed with a limp?"

"Yeap that's him." Nina said as she looked at Fifty for reassurance that Black Rob and Fifty wasn't good friends.

"Yeah, I now that bitch ass nigga, he beat my man out of ten pounds of weed back in the day." Fifty said to ease Nina's curiosity.

"Well, I know where his ass live, and I seen a big safe in his bedroom closet. He opened it one day when I was kicking it with him, and I was sitting on the bed and he went to grab me some money out of it, and it was filled with stacks of money. I don't know how much it was, but it was a lot!"

"That's the shit I'm talking about, I love a young down bitch!" Fifty said as Nina blushed at the compliment. "Where do this bitch ass nigga live at?"

"He got a nice house over off of Laffert Blvd. I know how to get there, but I can't tell you the exact street or address."

"Cool, will just roll over there after we leave here." Fifty said, "is this the only nigga that you know?"

"No, I use to fuck with this Italian dude name fat Tony. He was a little more discreet but one night we got drunk and he had to stop some where to pick up his cell phone, he took a black bag in with him that he got out of his trunk, and I believe that it was filled with money, because he was driving real conscious and mentioned that he'll be mad if he got pulled over by the police.

He tried to play it off like his friend lived at the house that he stopped at, but he used his key to open up the door. And one day, I was going to work late, and I seen him leaving with Susie AKA Cream, the white girl that dance with me at the club, and he took her to the same house. I just so happen to be getting dropped off by my home girl Nicky and we followed them.

When I asked him about it, he got mad and slapped the mess out of me, and called me a stupid nigger bitch. I don't go for no cracker calling me a nigger – it just sounds so disrespectful coming for them."

"I don't blame you! Where do he live?"

"The house that he went to was over on 235th street. I can show you where."

"Good!" The waitress brought their food and said, "If you need anything else just let me know, and I'll be right over."

"Thank you Maam." Fifty said with a smile as he stared at the Lobster and fried Oyster dinner. "Well baby after we get though eating, then we'll swoop by there and you can show me where these niggas live, and if they got it like you say, then we both should come off with a nice little come-up." Nina smiled with dollar signs in her eyes. Fifty knew that he had her, but he wanted to find out these two niggas location before he put the full court press down on her, cause then, she'll feel more obligated to him, and wouldn't want to lose out on her free lunch ticket.

* * * *

Summer was switching down the street when a nice brand new black Porsche pulled up along side her. The window rolled down as the Porsche rolled at a slow pace keeping up with Summer stroll. "Hey beautiful, are you looking for a man who likes to party?" The older white man asked.

"Maybe?" Summer said as she stopped and looked into the car.

"Well what would it cost me to get into the party." He said with a lustful smile.

"Well let me see what you're dancing with?" Summer said as the older white man pulled out his little dick and said "He's a good dancer too, but I got a different kind of desire."

"Oh yeah, what's that?" Summer asked. Then the white man pulled out a big black 12 inch dildo vibrator and held it up.

"I don't think so, that thing is too big for me!" Summer said knowing that the big dildo would probably tear her pussy all the way up, and fuck up her hustle.

"It's not for you, it's for me!" Said the white man, as Summer knew that he was most likely a married man who was probably in the closet.

"I can do that, but I'ma have to charge you extra – like $300.00 hundred dollars for thirty minutes of pleasure." Summer said.

"Deal!" The white man said with a smile.

"Pull into the motel up there and park and I'll take you to my room".

"O'kay," the white man sped off and pulled into the motel parking lot.

Summer walked into the parking lot and lead the tall old white man into her motel room. When she closed the door she said, "let me see that thing, damn, it's pretty big! Put the money on the table and get naked."

The white man dug in his pocket and put $300 hundred dollars on the table and started getting butt naked. Summer waited until he was naked, then went over to a bag and grabbed a douche and said, "I want you to go get clean, cause I'ma give it all to you!" She said with a smile as the white man smiled excitingly, and grabbed the douche and rushed into the bathroom.

Summer gave a wicked grin as she went through her tricks wallet and grabbed his platinum Visa card, and seen a stack of hundred dollar bills in it, and said "damn," to herself as she decided against taking it.

She looked at the man's name on his license and it said Jack Martin, and then she seen a business card slot and pulled one out, and the business card said Doctor Jack Martin Psychologist, and Summer took three of them, and put his wallet back and fixed his pants back, then stashed the credit card and business cards and got naked with only her high heels pumps on.

The white man opened up the door and walked out of the bathroom red in the face. He seen Summer's thick sexy body, and his dick jumped on impulse.

Summer said, "STOP, get on your damn knees and crawl your ass over here like the dog that you are."

The white man looked at Summer surprised and went to his knees as he crawled over to Summer.

Summer said, "kiss my shoe, and worship the baddest bitch that you ever seen."

Then as the white man started pecking her high hill pump, she said, "with your damn tongue – kiss it with your damn tongue!

Now get up on the bed and assume the position." He got up on the bed in a doggie position, as he looked back and watched Summer put the lubrication on the big black dildo vibrator and said, "and you better not scream either!"

Then she pressed the big dildo, into his ass and pushed it in halfway up in his ass, as he let out a small cry. "Did I tell you not to cry!" Summer said as she pulled his hair causing his head to come back, then she pushed the big dildo all the way up his ass and seen him clench his teeth as he turned as red as a tomato and Summer said, "you like that don't you," and she cut on the vibrator and started ramming him with it as she pulled his hair and he was going crazy like a gay nypho."

You like this bad black dick in your tight pussy huh you bitch?" And the white man shook his head as he started jacking himself off and coming all over his hand.

Summer told him to turn around and made him hold his legs up like a bitch, as she started talking to him nasty, and ramming him with the big dildo real hard, and he shook with his second orgasm as he screamed like a bitch and his body tightened up.

Summer went to go wash her hands and told him to go clean himself and his boy friend up. And he took his clothes and the dildo, and went to the bathroom to do as she said. Summer got dress, and grabbed her buck knife and slid it under the pillow, just in case he figured out that his credit card was missing and started acting crazy.

The white man walked out of the bathroom and said, "Beautiful, you're the best! I never had anyone who made me feel that good and alive in a long time."

"Here," and he gave her two more hundred dollar bills, and said, "I hope that I find you again, because you know how to please me like no one else."

"Well, if you ever come back through, then I'll be glad to give you what you desire." Summer said as she opened up the door and escorted him out.

Summer shut the door back and watched the black Porsche leave and she said, "DAMN....! He got this place smelling like shit, I got to clean this place up." She said as she started to clean up a little before she had to go back out and pull another trick. She thought, "My man is going to be proud of me, and know that I'm totally down and loyal to him." And she grabbed the credit card and her money and stuff, and took it to her other motel room to stash it.

* * * *

Fifty and Nina rolled by both of the two niggas spot that Nina put him up on. Fifty wrote down the street and address so he won't forget it.

As they were driving back, Fifty knew that he had to put the finishing touches on this game, so he pulled over and parked and cut the music down and said, "baby, this is a real big move for us both, because if I run in on him, and he tries to resist, then I might have to lay him down. I got to know that you're down for us, and a thorough bitch, because it's only a few ladies that I really trust, and know that they are down for me to the fullest, and that's my ladies that work for my escort service.

They hustle so we can eat good, and I respect them more because they hustle and play tricks for us, so we can live good and have the best in life. We know that these sucka's and tricks don't give a dame about us, that's why we play them out of their money ever chance we get. These are the bitches that I love, respect, and are totally down with, because they're real with me, and I'm the only man that they chose to love. I don't even have sex with a woman who's not part of my life, I know that my ladies only true desires is to please me. When I know that other women are just there to try to benefit off a cheap thrill, or see what they can get from a real nigga.

I like your looks and style Ma, but I question how down you really want to be with a true player?" And Fifty looked deep into Nina's sexy light brown eyes.

"Baby I want to be down with you to the fullest, I don't got no problems with getting my hustle on with a trick as long as I know that you will still respect and love me the same," Nina said.

"Shorty, how could I not, when I know that you're hustling for us! But also, you got to understand that I got two down woman's in my life that has earned the right to be considered my bottom bitches, and any woman who comes into my life got to respect and except them as such. They will respect you as my woman too, and be down with you like a sister's, because I don't tolerate that jealousy shit, and any woman that I bring home and except as my lady, will receive the equal love, loyalty, and respect as all my ladies do.

The reason for that is because we got the same interest, and desires at hand, and that is to play them sucka's like busters'. So if you really want to be down with me and my ladies, then you got to let me know. We'll still get money, but our association will be limited. I won't be able to respect and appreciate you as mine. So what's your desire?"

"I'm trying to be down with you all the way!" Nina said, with a shy smile.

"That's what I'm talking about, because I need a real and down bitch like you on my team. I know that you're a quality lady, and you know how to hustle these sucka and tricks." Nina smiled as Fifty lend over and gave her a passionate kiss on the lips, when his cell phone rung. He picked it up and answered it.

"Yo hello?"

"Hi daddy!"

"Hey baby, what's up?"

"Oh, I'm just getting this money and I wanted to tell you that I got that for you."

"Is that right? Baby I knew that you'd come through for your man, Listen, I'ma be there shortly o'kay!"

"O'kay daddy – I'll be waiting, love you!"

"You better love me Ma, cause if not, then I'ma be really disappointed." They laughed as Nina smiled and tried to hide her jealousy.

"O'kay bye."

"Bye, bye baby!" Fifty hung up and looked at Nina and said, "I apologize Ma, but your sister just put a lick together for me, and I got to go hit this lick before I miss this move. So can I come and hook up with you tomorrow after you get off from work, and we can make up for this lost time and finish putting our life's back in perspective?"

"Yeah Poppy, I understand! Nina said with a little sign of disappointment as Fifty pulled off and went to drop her off at her house.

He gave her a long passionate kiss and sent her on her way as he watched her sexy ass sway in them tight leather pants. He knew that he had to neglect her, so she won't think that her beauty or body was his addiction. She was the type of young bitch that niggas be jokin real hard, and she's used to using her body to tame niggas, and get them sprung. So to reject her only makes her try harder to please him. Fifty laughed as she waved and shut her door and he said, "Checkmate!" And drove off bumpin' Jay Z; The Reasonable Doubt CD as the song "I need dead presidents to represent me," was playing.

Chapter 11
Gamologist

Fifty went and spent the night with Summer and she loved every minute of his company. They talked and made slow passionate love all night, and Fifty put Summer up on Nina too, and Summer couldn't wait to meet her. Summer gave Fifty the Platinum Visa card and another regular Master Card that she stumbled across, and also gave Fifty the three business cards and $1,500 hundred dollars that she made in a short period of time. Fifty was impressed but didn't show it, and gave her back $300.00 dollars before he left in the morning, and told her to go to the beauty salon and get her hair and nails done. She agreed!

Fifty went to his town house and put on a nice dark blue silk Versace suit, and some dark blue gator boots to compliment his attire, and was off on a mission. He pulled up in the projects at 9:45a.m. and his three young comrades was up early getting their hustle on.

"Yo Sun, look at this nigga here! He looks like a fuckin attorney or executive or somebody." Baby Tank said as Fifty walked up.

"Yo Sun, you look fly kid, Yo – you're killin the game in that suit....that's you there Sun."

Fifty smiled as he greeted them all with their secret hand shake and said, "Yo Sun, we got to be versatile and have some class with our swag - feel me?"

That's right Sun, that's what I be telling these hard headed niggas, but they don't listen to game, these niggas is all jeans and T-shirts! Little G-nut said as he shook his head.

"Yo, fuck that kid! Yo Fifty, those are the cars that you requested parked over there," and Fifty looked over in the parking lot and seen the two buckets. "And it went down as smooth as you planned."

"Good, good, now listen! I need ya'll to assist me with some things today, because you guys is the only niggas that I trust."

"What's up Sun – we're down! What you need us to do?" Baby Tank asked.

"Listen, I need ya'll to go put on some khaki's and T-shirts and come and run some errands with me. I need ya'll to be my drivers as I put this game down and it would be sweet for us all."

"Cool, come on ya'll let's change!" Ra said to Baby Tank and Little G-nut, as they all walked into their apartment.

"Fifty said, call Juice and let him know that ya'll going to roll with me today and for him to keep the spot feed.

"Got you!" Ra said as he picked up the phone.

Fifty went to the check cashing store that his friend from high school worked at and she was happy to see him. She took a five hundred dollars cut off the five thousand dollars that he received from the Platinum Visa, and three hundred dollars off the plan Master card that Fifty only was able to pull $1,500 hundred dollars off of, so Fifty received $4,450 dollars off both credit cards.

Fifty left there and went to rent three big U-haul trucks, and had the youngsters caravan in back of him as he pulled up to another nice and expensive furniture store.

Fifty put on his gold frame glasses and told Ra to come with him, and Baby Tank and Little G-nut to stay with the trucks, as he and Ra went inside.

An old white lady approached as Fifty said, "Hello Maam, my name is Dr. Martin," and he handed the lady a business card and said, and I just brought a new mansion in Jamaica Gardens, and I was looking for some luxurious furniture to compliment my new home."

"Oh, well Sir – you certainly came to the right place," the lady said, we got some of the finest leather furniture that money can buy.

"I see!" Fifty said as he rubbed the Italian soft leather couch. "Oooowow, I like that!"

"What's that Sir?"

"The burgundy leather corner group set! Oooowow and I like that too....the butter taffy leather sofa, love seat and double chair set. I want them both, and I'll take those tables right there, and those too, and that electric audio cabinet that rise up and the stand, and those matching table too. And give me that big dinning room table – the one that sits 12 people. And I'll take those blue couches too, and the blue tables that match. Also, I want 4 of those dark blue leather chairs and 4 dark blue lazy boy chairs. O'kay now I need some bedroom sets.

"Over here Sir!" The lady said as she lead Fifty over toward the bedroom set area.

"O'kay, give me that big black king size bedroom set, and six of those twin size beds all different colors, and dressers to match. Yeah that should do it for now, how much do I owe you for all this?"

The lady grabbed her calculator and said, "$46,000 thousand dollars Sir!"

"O'kay here," Fifty went into his new Eel skin wallet and handed her the Platinum Master card and she ran off to go charge all the stuff up without another word.

Ra looked at Fifty and said, "Yo Sun, you're an animal for real!" And they laughed.

The lady came back with the receipt and Fifty signed it, and told her that he already hired the services of a professional moving company, and trucks was parked outside. So she had her workers load the three big U-haul trucks up and they were off. Fifty took them to his new baby mansion and they went crazy as they run around looking through the place. Fifty told them about his new escort service, and that his ladies was going to stay in the house with him, and they just embraced Fifty with their utmost respect and admiration.

Fifty had them unload the first truck, and he had little G-nut to drive him to the circuit city that his partner from high school worked at.

"Hey Fifty, what's up player! Yo, much love Sun, keeping it 100% with me."

"Yo Sun that's what real niggas do! But listen, I'm trying to do it again."

"Word!" Fifty shook his head. "Yo, let's do it Sun, I'm down!"

And Fifty smiled and went on a serious buying spree. He grabbed two big 70 inch TV's, three big 60 inch TV's, six 19 inch TV's, three new JVC stereo systems, six nice Sony small CD stereo systems, a washer and dryer, a big black refrigerator, a deep freezer, and stove, also a microwave, computer, camcorder, four DVD's and a complete home stereo theater system.

Fifty's old high school friend grabbed a washer and dryer and a computer for himself. And ran to go charge everything up, it all went through like clock work, and Fifty and Little G-nut was headed back to the mansion.

Fifty made a stop at the hardware store, and brought some tools so they could put all the stuff together easier. Then they stopped and grabbed a bucket of chicken and a 12 pack of beer, then headed back to the mansion.

Ra and Baby Tank had all the furniture unloaded when Fifty and Little G-nut got back, and Fifty told them where he wanted everything, and that the dark blue leather couches, a 60 inch TV and a JVC stereo system was for them, and they was really feeling that. Fifty told them to put his partner's washer and dryer, and computer to the side, and then took Baby Tank with him as they headed to the Green Aches Mall.

When they arrived, Fifty went into Robinson May and brought all of the quilts, sheets, towels, pots, pans, microwave bowls, dishes, silverwares, and glasses. Then he went to the ladies section and brought twenty baby doll outfits, twenty fancy name brand sexy lingerie, and ten sexy G-string bathing suits.

He grabbed ten different kinds of perfumes and ten different kinds of Victoria Secret feminine body wash kits. After taking that stuff to the truck Fifty went to his Italian partner who owns the popular clothing store, and he had Baby Tank pick out five sweat suits, five pair of jeans, three pairs of shoes, and five shirts and two coats for all of his comrades. And Baby Tank didn't miss a beat.

He knew all of his comrade's sizes and style and put it together like an urban model. Fifty grabbed Summer five new Donna Karen dresses, three pair of Gator Stilettos, five Nautica sweat suits, and four sexy leather outfits – two pants and two skirt outfits with matching tops. It all came up to $38,000 thousand dollars and the Visa card worked like magic. Fifty and Baby Tank was out like a light, as they went to the closest Ralph supermarket and charged the Master card up with $2,600 hundred dollars worth of food, cosmetics, and alcohol.

They laughed all the way to the mansion as they walked in, and heard the music bumping and Ra and Little G-nut was putting the finishing touches on the bedroom sets. Fifty and Baby Tank started grabbing all the other stuff out of the truck that they just brought, and when Ra and little G-nut seen all of their fly gear, they went nuts with excitement.

An hour later, everything was pretty much put in place, so Fifty had them put their stuff back on the truck and Baby Tank, and Little G-nut went to take their stuff home, as Fifty had Ra follow him over to his partner that work at Circuit City apartment, and they unloaded his stuff.

When Fifty and Ra arrived back at the projects, Little G-nut and Baby Tank had all of their stuff put in their apartment, and Juice was raving over his fly gear. The youngsters told him how Fifty put it down with the credit cards, and they all shared a good laugh. Then they told Juice about the mansion and Juice couldn't wait to see it. It was 9:15p.m. and Fifty had the youngsters follow him to drop the U-haul trucks off, then he dropped them back off and told them to be ready tomorrow, because it's G-day! They all agreed excitedly as Fifty rolled out.

Fifty arrived at the Q-motel at 10:00 o'clock and Summer was walking out of her motel room when she seen him pull up. "Hey Ma, where you going?"

"Hi daddy, I was just about to go to work," Summer said.

"You haven't been out working yet," Fifty asked as Summer looked kind of confused, not knowing if Fifty was going to be mad at her for not going to work earlier or what......?

She said, "no baby, I was kind of tired!"

"Are you tired now?" Fifty asked.

"No, I'm good now!" Summer stated with a little hesitation in her voice.

"Good, so would you like to roll with me tonight?"

"Her eyes lit up," I would love to baby!" Summer said with a bright smile on her face.

"Good, but first come and grab these bags out of the trunk for me." And Fifty popped the trunk as they grabbed all the bags and took them into the motel room.

"I got these for you Ma, I hope you like them."

"Fo real baby!" Summer yelled with excitement.

"Of course, you know that I got to keep my bottom lady fly, you're a reflection of me baby."

"Oh, thank you baby," she gave him a big hug and kiss and started looking through all of her fly gear acting like a little kid in a toy store.

"Well, go and get fly so we can roll!" Summer smiled and rushed to the bathroom to shower and get fly.

Fifty got on the phone and called Tee-Tee, and when she answered, she was glad to hear from him. He told her that he would be over to pick her up in twenty minutes, and for her to be ready, Fifty, smiled as he hung up the phone.

* * * *

Fifty and Summer arrived at Tee Tee's brick apartment complex and Tee-Tee was standing out front waiting, and dress to impress. When she noticed Fifty in the black Cadillac Seville, she was all smiles, but was briefly surprised when she noticed another lady sitting in the passenger seat. Fifty got out of the car and walked around to her and gave her a big passionate kiss, and it eased her thoughts, as Fifty opened up the passenger door and said Tee-Tee this is your sister Summer, Summer this is your sister Tee-Tee," and both of the ladies smiled and giggled.

Summer said, "it's a pleasure to finally meet you, daddy talks highly of you," and she step out of the car and gave Tee-Tee a small hug to break the ice.

"Thank you! He speaks very fond of you as well," Tee-Tee said as they giggled and got back into the car. Tee-Tee jumped in the back seat and Summer turned in her seat as Fifty pulled off. Then they started talking as if they knew each other all their life. Fifty smiled to him self and said, "Checkmate."

Fifty drove them to a fancy Italian restaurant that was open late night, and as they got out of the car, Fifty could see both of the ladies sizing each-other up. Both was super fine and had body for days. Tee-Tee was only two inches taller then Summer standing about five foot, six inches, and had a sexy fat heart shaped ass, as Summer had a fat ghetto butty. Both had a small waste and thick hips and thighs, and both had a perfectly shaped breast, but Tee-Tee's was just maybe a size bigger, she was a beautiful cream complexion sista' with wavy sandy-brown hair and beautiful light brown bedroom eyes.

Summer on the other hand, was a beautiful red bone sista' with a couple of cute small freckles on her cheeks, and a face that any woman would kill for, she had her hair cut into a short sexy Toni Braxton hair cut, and was killin the game. Both of them intertwined their arms though Fifty's arms, as they all walked side-by-side into the restaurant. Fifty felt all eyes on him, as he step through the door with two of the baddest bitches in the game. They all talked and ate for an hour or so, and Fifty knew that they were the perfect match for one another.

"Listen ladies, this is where the game gets deep at, you both know my expectations of you. (And Fifty looked at Summer then back at Tee-Tee.) You both are considered my bottom ladies from now on, and it's us against the muthafucken world. Other bitches will come into our life and some will get dismissed, and some will end up leaving, but no matter what, from now on, you two are my two down and thorough ride or die bitches, and I believe in you, and have trust that you two can represent me and our cause to the fullest. The other bitches that will be accepted into our family are under your responsibility and respectful authority. Not like a pimp, but more like a big sister who's down for them, and who will always keep it real with them. Your job is to lace them, and make sure that they're taken care of and most of all that they go out to clubs, concerts, comedy clubs, business and political conventions and so on, to weed out the good clientele, and build a good net work of rich and elite tricks. It's time to elevate this game to another level, and I expect you two to build me a crew of down, beautiful, and thorough bitches who knows how to get that money, and stay committed to our cause, as well as devoted to pleasing me!

Jealousy is not apart of our lives, and you two must respect the love and desire that your other sisters will have for wanting to please me. You both should know me good enough by now, and understand the type of man that you got in your life, and should know how to play your position to the fullest. If you ever try to intentionally disrespect me, or try to deceive me, then I will dismiss your ass with no hesitation.

Now, if you don't think that you qualify for this position in your life, or can't deal with the rules, laws, and authority, then you can walk away now, and there won't be no hard feelings." Tee-Tee looked over at Summer and Summer looked at Tee-Tee, then they both looked at Fifty.

"I'm down for us daddy." Summer said.

"I wouldn't think about leaving you, and I'm down for you both to the fullest." Tee-Tee said with a sincere smile.

Fifty pulled out two beautiful four carat diamond ankle bracelets, and got up and clipped them on both of the ladies right ankles and said, "let every step that you take be for me, us, and our cause, because it's us against the world now ladies, and if a person ain't with us, then they're against us. And being that this day marks a special moment in our life, then it's only right that a kiss should compliment this marriage, so give your sister a kiss and display your love and loyalty to her. Summer lend over and gave Tee-Tee a passionate kiss, and it was obvious that they both was bi-sexual from the way they enjoyed it. When they stopped Fifty lend over and kissed Tee- Tee, then Summer, and the bound was close, locked, and sealed!

Fifty put a hundred dollar bill on the table and they left out.

It was 12:45a.m. when Fifty pulled into his new baby mansion, and the steal gates was left open so Fifty just drove in and pulled up to the front of the mansion as he parked in the beautiful brick circular driveway.

Summer said, Damn daddy, this is nice, who lives here?"

"This belongs to a very good friend of mine, and he heard about my escort service and asked me if I would bring some of my ladies by to party with him. So I want ya'll to go and fuck his brains out, and let him know that I got the baddest bitches in the game. Ya'll down with that?"

"Of course daddy, whatever you want!" Summer said.

"Yeah daddy I'm down!" Tee-Tee said with a little smile, trying not to seem to disappointed, because she wanted to kick it with Fifty tonight, not some stranger! But she knew that this was the life that she has chose, so she would do whatever it took to please her man and be down with him.

They existed the car and walked up to the front door as Fifty pulled out his key and unlocked the door.

"He gave you a key too?" Summer asked in a surprised manner.

"Yeap!" Fifty said as he opened up the door and they walked in and the ladies was looking around the big beautiful mansion in a captivating way.

"This is beautiful!" Summer said.

"You ain't lying sis, this house is like heaven!" Tee-Tee said.

"Ya'll like it?" Fifty asked.

"Hell yeah!" Summer flatly stated.

"Good, welcome home then Ma!" They both looked at Fifty with a surprised look on their face.

"Quit playing!" Summer said.

"Nah Ma, I ain't playing, this is our new house – what you think, we're going to live in a motel or the projects, hell naw Ma, it's nothing but the best for me and mine's."

Tee-Tee and Summer started screaming as if they were on the Price is Right and started hugging Fifty and each other.

"Come on let me show you around," and Fifty took them up stairs to the master bedroom and said, "This is our room, and I want both of my ladies to share my bed with me too. You ladies don't have a problem with that do you?"

"Hell naw baby, I would want nothing less." Tee-Tee said.

"Me either daddy!"

"Good come on – now these are the other bedrooms for the other ladies that we bring home, we got six extra rooms for our other ladies, so I'm sure that eight ladies should be able to effectively run the escort service to start off with, now come on, and Fifty escorted them down stairs to the living room and family room, and said, "as you see, I took the liberty in pimpin' it out, thanks to my baby girl Ms. Summer."

"And she blushed and said, "it looks real nice daddy, you got good taste!"

"So I've been told!" Fifty said as he slapped Tee-Tee on the ass, and they laughed.

"Come look at this," and he took them to the room that was converted with the proper state of the art home theater hook up.

"Now this is what I'm talking about, this place is off the hook!" Tee-Tee said as she looked around and marveled at the beautiful setting.

"I never seen nothin' as fly as this in my life daddy." Summer said as she grabbed Fifty's hand and kissed the back of it." Thank you so much, I don't know what to say!"

"You both said it all when I seen that devoted look in your eyes, what's more is it to say?" Fifty said as he lend over and gave Summer a passionate kiss, and when they stopped, Tee-Tee walked up and kissed him too, and said, "you know that we both are madly in love with you!"

"I think that the feelings mutual Ma! Now come on and let me show you both the Pool, Jacuzzi and Tennis Court!"

"You're kidding, we got a tennis court too?" Tee-Tee asked excitingly.

"Yeap, and a basketball court!

Fifty and the ladies stayed up all night getting the mansion together. They had to make up beds, put away the food, and dishes and stuff, and clean, decorated, and sanitize the bathrooms and kitchen. It was 5:00a.m. when they finished, and they spent the next two hours sexually satisfying one another, and it was no question that Fifty had two of the freakiest ladies in the game.

They woke up at two that afternoon, and went to grab something to eat, then Fifty went to rent them a new blue Cadillac Escalade truck, and gave them both a key to the mansion and security codes, and $5,000 thousand dollars a piece, and told them to go shopping to get themselves some new clothes, so they could always look fly. Then they kissed and departed as Fifty jumped in the Seville with revenge on his mind.

Chapter 12
Let the Games Begin

It was 8:30p.m. when fifty pulled up at the Guy Brewer projects and jump out of his old school Cutless, he was dressed in some black Guess jeans, black hoody sweat shirt, with some black Cortez Nikes, and a all black New York fitted baseball cap. He walked up to the youngsters apartment door and knocked, as Baby Tank looked out of the peep hole and opened the door, and welcomed his comrade with their secret hand shake. Fifty walked in and every one of his comrades was dressed with black khaki suits on, and black tennis shoes. Fifty smiled as he seen how the new furniture and audio set up made the whole apartment look better as he heard Tupac's, Thug Life CD echoing though the apartment at a nice low volume. Fifty gave all of his comrades a hand shake and said, "Are ya'll ready to flirt with death?"

"It seem like that's been a regular part of our struggles, so ain't no sense in duckin it now Sun!" Ra said, as Juice threw a duffle bag on the table, and put on his brownie gloves and started pulling out all kinds of new guns.

"Yo Sun, he only had 3 silencers for the Gloc's, so I got three 3.80's with the silencer hook up, and I grabbed these two Mac lls and this Tec 9 with a silencer, just in case we have to go hard. Also, we got extra clips for all of them, and I brought some boxes of hollo points and loaded them all up already for us. Oh and here's the other stuff that little

G-nut went to get from that list you gave him." And juice pulled out some ski mask, brownie gloves, a scanner, and four two way walkie-talkies, and a little bundle of black plastic straps.

141

"Beautiful, I know that you guys was on top of your game. Now peep, I got the scoop on where these niggas live at, and I plan on trying to get these niggas for their worth too, so we can enjoy the spoils of war. So try not to be too quick to kill, because we won't be able to open up the safes without the combination, so let's try to move quick and right. Now I've scoped out the neighborhoods and houses, and this is how I believe we should put it down." And Fifty started telling them the plan as they plotted the hit.

* * * *

Fifty and Little G-nut pulled up down the street from Red's proper four bedroom house in the brown 76 Malubu, and Juice followed him and parked further down on the opposite side of the street with Ra and Baby Tank in the 79 Buick Skylark. It was 11:30p.m. and the block was quiet and still, as Fifty and Little G-nut crept up Red's driveway passed his Red Vett, and his new Red 500 Benz Coup. They walked up to the fence and a big black pit bull started growling at them and Little G-nut shot it in the head with the Gloc 9mm with the silencer. Fifty looked over at him and he said, "I always wanted to do that!" And Fifty shook his head, as he opened up the fence and grabbed the dead dog by his hind legs, and drug it and threw it in the bushes.

Fifty had a walkie-talkie on him, and Juice had the scanner and the other three with him. Juice hit the button and Fifty whisper, "Yo, what's up"!

"Ra, is on the way!" Juice said.

"Clear!" Fifty responded and then he whispered too Little G-nut and told him. Then they made their way around the house looking through each window. Ra caught up with them, and Fifty held his finger up telling Ra to be quiet, and then glanced through the back door window and seen Red in the kitchen cooking up some dope. Red was shaking his head to the beat as Jadakiss CD was bumping through the stereo system at a nice loud tone. Fifty seen three keys cooked up on the table, and two more on the counter still wrapped up, with the scale, baking soda, and some B-12 next to it. Fifty knew why his dope was garbage then, and wondered if he'll get an opportunity to creep in before Red finish cooking up the rest of the dope. Fifty went to the back of Reds back yard and hit Juice on the walkie-talkie.

"Yo G!"

"What's up G!"

"My tire is flat, I need a crow bar!"

"Got you Rade!"

Fifty waited as the walkie-talkie clicked and Fifty said, "What's up G?"

"Yo B is on the way to help you, every thing is good on my end!"

"Cool-out!" Fifty uttered as he crept back by Ra and Little G-nut, and he said, Baby Tank is on the way!"

Then a minute later Baby Tank crept from around the house with the crow bar and gave it to Fifty. All of them pulled down their ski mask and waited for their opportunity to make their move.

Fifty heard the song go off and the phone rang as Red stop mixing the dope and ran to the phone. Then another song came on and Fifty put the crow bar in the crack of the door, and popped it open with ease, as they ran into Reds house quick and swift, and Fifty seen Reds back slightly turned as Fifty ran up to him full speed while he was on the phone and when Red caught a glimpse of the person running up behind him, he was stuck as Fifty slapped him across the face with the crow bar, and knocked him unconscious. Fifty picked up the phone off the carpet and hung it up. Then he search Red and had little G-nut bound his legs and hands up with the plastic restraints.

Fifty hit the walkie-talkie and said, "The party has begun!"

Then Juice said, "I got you –out!"

Fifty looked at the dope and shook his head, and put the one and a half kilo's that wasn't touched yet, in a separate bag from the other dope that Red had already cut and cooked up.

"He's woke!" Little G-nut said, as he stood over Red smiling through his ski mask.

Fifty walked over to him as the blood from his swollen face drenched the rug. Ra and Baby Tank came from the hallway from checking the bedrooms and said, "They're clear! But it's a big safe in the master bedroom," and Ra dropped a black leather sports bag at Fifty's feet.

"What's that?"

"Dope, five keys untouched!" Ra said with a smile.

"Yo Sun, look like you ran into a bad day!" Fifty said! "Either you can die and keep the money in your safe, or you can live and be able to hustle another day! It's up to you?"

"Go fuck yourself!"

"O'kay you want to play the hard way huh! I'm cool with that."

"Yo go grab me a knife out of the kitchen." And Baby Tank smiled and went to grab a big Jason knife and handed it to Fifty.

"O'kay, I tell you what, either you give me the combination, or I'ma cut off your dick off and make you a bitch for life!" Fifty turned Red on his back and pulled down his sweat pants and grabbed hold of his dick with the gloves on, and put the big Jason knife against his dick, and Red said, "O'kay, O'kay, please don't do me like that- you can have the money! The combination is 1-8-7!"

Fifty looked at Ra and Little G-nut and said, "Go check it out!" They ran to the back and a minute later Little G-nut came back out and said, "it's right!"

Fifty looked at Red and said, "Do you know who we are, and why we are here?"

"Naw man, just take the money and please go, I don't care who you are!"

"It's not that easy Sun, you disrespected us and my bitch-you raped her and forced her to do things that was indecent, and now it's time to pay for your bad deeds. Tell my homies in hell that I send my love!" He looked at Baby tank and said, "Send this bitch ass nigga to hell!" And Baby Tank smiled and shot Red twice in the head and three times in the heart. Ra came out of the bedroom with Little G-nut carrying a suit case and Little G-nut had a duffle bag and a AK-47 wrapped in a black Mink coat.

"What's in the bag?" Fifty asked Little G-nut.

"Just guns, weed, and jewelry! That's all" Baby Tank heard jewelry and reached down and took off Reds Fat diamond Rolex chain, watch, and ring, and looked at Fifty and said, "he's not going to need this where he's at!" Fifty shook his head as he grabbed a half of kilo of the cut dope, and hide it in the freezer.

"Why you doing that?" Little G-nut asked.

"Because when the police come and find this nigga, they will find the dope too, and consider the murder drug related, and that would put a quick end to the investigation.

"Wow, that's smart!" Ra said, as they crept back out and Tupac song, "Hell Mary", came on and bumped through the stereo system.

* * * *

Fifty and the youngsters took their profit and gains to the youngster's apartment, and then went to go finish their mission.

Big Pain and Rock was in the spot pullin' a train on this big butt dark skin smoker bitch name Pam, with five other niggas kicking back playing with their play station awaiting their turn, when they heard the car alarm go off on Rocks brand new Lexus 300 sitting on 20" chrome Lorenzo's. Rock pulled his dick out of the dark skin base head bitch mouth, and pulled up his pants, grabbed his 357 magnum and run out of the house with Bandit and big lip Ed running right behind him. Face seen Rock run out of the bedroom, and he went into the bedroom and put his dick in the smoker bitch mouth while Big Pain was hitting her from the back. Mo and Jim Jim just continue to play Madden Football and smoken weed. Rock seen a big ass brick on top of his hood, and his front windshield busted, "What the fuck", he said, as he cut off his alarm.

Bandit and Big lip Ed started bustin up and Bandit said, "It looks like Cindy's mad at your scandalous ass!" And him and Big lip Ed started bustin up.

"I'ma kill that crazy bitch - watch!" Rock said, as three silent bullets flew through the air and hit Rock dead off in the chest and dropped him dead. Bandit said, "What the Fu......!" and his words was cut off as him and Big lip Ed both got hit three times in the body. Rock was holding his stomach in shock as a shadow stood over him and shot him twice in the head. Big lip Ed was twisted on his stomach laying face down when Ra shot him in the back of the head for good measures, and shot Bandit too before he walked in the house.

Mo said, "aaahh nigga your burned", and looked to his side and seen half of Jim-Jim face gone, and the blood splattered all over the TV leaving Mo laying face down on the dirty carpet.

When the door busted open to the bedroom the first bullet hit Pam in the hip, causing her to bit half of Face dick off as Face cried out in pain, and Big Pain looked up and caught three bullets to his side and stumbled back a couple of steps, then rushed at Baby Tank full speed as Baby Tank unloaded ten shots into Big Pains upper body dropping him at Baby Tanks feet. Face was sitting on the ground with his back against the wall holding his dick with fear in his eyes. As Baby Tank unloaded the rest of his clip in Face head, leaving the wall painted with Face's blood.

Pam was lying on the bed butt naked holding her hip, and crying as she said, "please don't kill me, I'll do whatever you want." Ra walked in as she pleaded for her life, and he shot her twice in the head. Tank looked over at his comrade and seen death in his eyes, as Baby Tank reloaded his gloc.

Ra and Baby Tank walked into the room where Fifty was, and seen the two niggas dead with their brains blown out and the TV had the video game on pause displaying a touch down sign, as blood dripped down the screen. Ra said, "Remind me to get rid of that Sega Genesis," and Baby Tank shook his head as Fifty laughed. Little G-nut walked in the room with them and said, "Damn, I guess no one won!" And they started laughing as he said, "I found this nine ounces on the dresser".

Fifty said, "go put it in the cabinet and let's roll, we got to finish this shit!" Little G-nut did what he said, as they crept out undetected.

* * * *

Crime was in his shower getting the rest of Michelle pussy scent off of him when he turned the water off and stepped out to grab the towel, and seen his worst nightmare staring him in the face, two niggas with guns and ski mask on. "I advise you to lay your big black ass on the floor before I shoot the shit out of you." Fifty uttered.

"Okay man, you caught me slippin-just don't kill me, you can have what-ever you want." Crime said as he laid down on the cold tile in the bathroom floor.

Fifty looked at Ra and said, "tie him up!"

Ra went to go try to tie him up and Crime tried to jump up and grab Ra's gun up out of his waste band, and

Fifty socked Crime in the jaw with a hard jab, dropping him back to his knees as Ra kicked him dead off in the face with his black Tims knocking Crime unconscious.

Crime woke up and seen his bitch Michelle butt naked tide up on the floor ten feet away from him on his bedroom floor, but she was blind folded.

"Listen, give us the combination to the safe or we're going to kill your bitch!" Fifty said knowing that Crime didn't give a damn about no bitch.

"Why should I give it to you – you're just going to kill us any-way, so just get it over with."

"What......? Please don't hurt us, Crime just give them the fuckin combination." Michelle screamed!

"Shut up bitch – they're just going to kill your dumb ass any-way!"

"No we're not, we don't have to kill you it's up to you, either you can give us the combination and tell us where's the dope at, or we can kill you and carry this safe out of here – it's not that big and it's not bolted down, so make it light on yourself?" Fifty said as he seen Crime eyes wonder, knowing that he was weighing his options. Being that the safe was small enough to be carried out did change Crime's focus, because they could easily just kill him and take the damn safe any-way, so he had to give it to them and hope that they won't kill him any-way.

"It's 5-9-11....!"

And Ra went to go open up the safe and said, "it's good."

"See that wasn't hard; now tell me where is the dope at?" Fifty asked.

"It's in the other bedroom in the blue duffle bag, back at the top of the shelf." Then Baby Tank went to go retrieve it, and came back with a duffle bag and two big zip lock plastic bag full of ounces. "How much is that?" Fifty asked.

"About 180 ounces!" Crime said. Little G-nut reached down and took off Crimes Rolex watch, chain, and 3 carat diamond ring and said, "let me get this off you playboy." And Crime frowned up at him. "OH, you got me scared, can I kill him?" Little G-nut asked as Crime facial expression changed, and he turned and looked up at Fifty.

"Naw, I got something else in store for him." Then Fifty took one of Crimes dirty socks and stuffed it in Crimes mouth, and tied the other one around his head to hold the sock in place. He looked at Juice and said "I want you and Ra to take the stuff and meet us at the spot, we'll be their shortly. "I need you two" and he gestured toward Little G-nut and Baby Tank, "to help me take this nigga somewhere, so he can be properly dealt with."

"What about her?" Ra asked.

"Do you think that she's a threat?"

"Hell yeah she's a threat……!" Ra uttered with assurance.

"I don't know who you are, and I won't say nothing if you let me go – I promise! Please don't kill me, please!" Michelle cried.

"Yo Sun, fuck this bitch – tears don't move me." Ra argued and Fifty looked at Juice and then Baby Tank, and they just threw their hands up like they didn't know what to do!

"Listen Sun, this bitch could put us away for life!" Ra stated with persistence.

"I feel you Sun – it's your call then." Fifty said as Ra looked over at the lady and shot her twice in the head with no remorse.

Crime looked up at Fifty with tears in his eyes, knowing that his death was drawing near.

Baby Tank and Little G-nut knocked Crime out and drugged him to Crimes new Ford Excursion, and put him in the back seat then followed Fifty.

Fifty got on his cell phone and made a call, and then pulled up in this alley in back of some vacant houses. Ten minute later Tee-Tee jumped out of the Cadillac Escalade, and walked up around the corner to the alley as she seen Fifty dressed in all black standing next to this young light skin guy. "Damn, she's like that Sun." Little G-nut said as he admired Tee-Tee beautiful appearance.

"What's up daddy?" Tee-Tee asked curiously.

"I got a little surprise for you Ma," and Fifty opened up the back door to the Ford Excursion and Crime was laid on his side curled up with his eye bruised and the side of is face swollen. Fifty looked over at Baby Tank.

"Yo sun, he tried me, so I gave him what he asked for!" Baby Tank said.

Tee-Tee laughed and said, "remember me you sick son-of-a-bitch, now it's my turn to dog you!"

Fifty handed Tee-Tee the gloc with the silencer that he had. Baby Tank said, "Wait bitch! Yo, let me move out of the way," and he jumped out of the truck, as everyone started laughing except Crime.

Crime looked at Tee-Tee with tears in his eyes and Little G-nut said, "Yo Ma, we ain't got all damn-night-handle your business, or get out of the fuckin way."

She looked at little G-nut, then back at Crime, and lifted the Gloc 9mm and as soon as Crime looked her in the eyes, she let off ten shots right into his forehead and face, removing any trace of his appearance.

"Damn, now that's what I call over kill…!" Baby Tank said as Fifty closed the back door to the truck.

"Yo Ma's, a down bitch rade! I like her!" Little G-nut said, as Fifty smiled and took the gun from Tee-Tee and gave her a big kiss and said, "You Alright?" She shook her head yes, and Fifty said, "I'll be home in a couple of hours o'kay!"

"O'kay," Tee-Tee said as she left.

Fifty jumped in the Malubu with the youngsters and put the gun that Tee-Tee used in a plastic bag, so he could bury it with Tee-Tee's finger prints on it, just in case she tried to cross him up in the end, he'll have something on her to make her think twice about it. Fifty smiled at his devilish thought as he drove off.

Everyone was back at the apartment cleaned up and celebrating as Juice, Ra, Baby Tank, and Little G-nut counted the money and Fifty re-cooked the dope trying to cook most of the cut off of it. He had to re-melt it down, and then take the uncut cocaine and mix it with the rock cocaine that's already been cooked, and he mixed a half shot of Bacardi 151 light with the water, to make the dope give off the strong heated effect so when the smokers tasted it, they start to sweat, because the alcohol opens up their pores. He put 9 ounces of good with 18 ounces of the dope that had already been cut and cooked up. That way he could bring back 22 ounces after cooking off the cut. Fifty cooked up the 7 kilos that had the cut on it, and mixed it with 3 kilos of the good dope that was untouched, and only came back with 8½ kilos of better shit, and still had 4 kilos of good powder cocaine put to the side.

Juice said, "Yo Fifty, we got $630,000 thousand dollars Rade! That's a $126,000 thousand a piece!" And everyone smiled as the youngsters barely could contain their joy.

"Listen, we need to just continue to sell rocks so we can build our clientele up good, and have this spot poppin, and then we can start recruiting workers to work for us out of our spot." Juice said.

"Yeah, because you know that our clientele is about to pick up big time now that Reds gone!" Baby Tank added.

"Yo Sun, I don't want none of ya'll mentioning this to nobody, this shit stays right here between us five, until death! Do ya'll understand?" Fifty said.

"Yeah, we got you Rade, we don't go around doing no bragging!" Little G-nut said in their defense.

"Good, and make sure that ya'll throw away them damn guns, dispose of them for good, we don't need any slip up's or foolish mistakes that can take us down, so keep your game tight. And I think that we should split the profit to the dope five ways too, so ya'll can just put mine to the side – all I want is $500 hundred on an ounce, so you guys can have the extra for slangin it. Deal?"

"That shit sounds good to us!" Baby Tank said.

"O'kay off this 12½ keys ya'll only owe me $45,000 thousand and the rest is ya'lls to split.

"Good looking out Rade – also can you hold them other four keys for us until we finish the shit that's already cooked?" Juice asked.

"Of course – I got ya'll...!"

They laughed and talked for an hour more, then Fifty left and went to take the four kilo's and money to his town house apartment, then he showered and packed some clothes and headed for the mansion.

When Fifty arrived at the mansion it was 5:15a.m. the next morning and as Fifty walked in the door, he was greeted by his two beautiful soul-mates.

"Yo what's up Ma? I thought that ya'll would be sound asleep dreaming of me." He said as Tee-Tee and Summer rushed into his arms and gave him a big hug and kiss.

"Baby you know that I was worried about you!" Tee-Tee firmly stated.

"Ma, I'ma Gorilla – you know us silver backs run the jungle." And they smiled together.

Summer said, "Daddy, what's going on? Tee-Tee won't tell me, and my curiosity is killing me!"

"Well baby, I told Tee-Tee not to mention our situation to nobody, and It's best that you don't know certain things that me and Tee-Tee deal with, and sometimes Tee-Tee won't know some of the things that me and you put down. So don't allow silent mysteries to irritate your thoughts, you know what type of man that I am, and you know that I will always protect you, and have your back, whether right or wrong. You feel me Ma?"

"Yeah daddy I feel you!"

"Good, now how about cooking me some breakfast, because I'm starving – can ya'll cook?"

"Of course baby," Tee-Tee said.

"I know enough to satisfy my man, but I'm no five star chief or nothing." Summer said as they laughed, and the ladies went to prepare their man a big breakfast.

Fifty went to put his clothes in the bedroom, then went into the family room and watched the news. The news was broadcasting footage of the blue Ford Excursion truck with the yellow tape around it, when Tee-Tee walked into the family room and sat right next to Fifty, cuddling up on him like a little girl would do her father.

Then the news flipped to the scene that was at the hang out spot, and white sheets was covering up bodies in the yard, as the yellow tape had the whole area of the yard taped off. The headlines at the bottom said eight people dead in a drug war shooting.

Tee-Tee looked over at Fifty and kissed him on the neck and said, "I love you so much baby, and thank you for being down for me. I'm your ride or die bitch for life!"

"I know!" Fifty uttered with a smile.

"What about Red? You know that he's going to act a fool once he hears about his crew." Tee-Tee asked inquisitively.

"Well let's just say that, we won't have to worry about that nigga getting mad." And Fifty and Tee-Tee shared a good laugh together.

Fifty decided to spend some quality time with his beautiful soul-mates. They spent three whole nights and days together enjoying good sex and having fun, as they went all over the place together. The first day, they went to the Museum of Natural History in Manhattan, and then shot over to see funny man Bernie Mac do his thang at the Apollo Theater. Bernie Mac had the crowd laughing with tears coming out of their eyes as he put down his unforgettable performance. They all enjoyed the show, and laughed about it all the way home.

The next day Fifty took the ladies to the Great Adventure in New Jersey, and they had a ball taking pictures and jumping on ride-after-ride.

The third day they went to Reese Beach, and walked the beach hand and hand as they enjoyed the nice warmth of the hot sun rays, and they indulged in each others profound thought's and desires. It was a day well spent, as they made it home at 6:00p.m. and Fifty told them both that he wanted them to walk around naked for the rest of the day, and they all walked around in their glory as Fifty took pictures and fucked all night.

Chapter 13
Grinding

As soon as Fifty pulled up to the Guy Brewer projects, he seen smokers everywhere – running here, there, jumping in and out of cars, and some was even posted up as look outs. Fifty pulled into the parking lot and seen two brand new Escalade trucks one was burgundy sitting on some nice 20 inch chrome rims, and the other one was cream sitting on some nice different 20 inch chrome rims. Off to the side of them, was a brand new bad ass platinum color 500 Benz coup sitting on some 20 inch Ashanta's, and in the back of the parking lot was a off white with gold trimming Lincoln Navigator sitting on gold 20 inch Daton wire rims with off white spokes. Fifty shook his head as he gave a understanding grin, knowing that his little comrades never really had nothing, and now it was their turn to shine.

"Yo Sun, what's up B!" Ra said as he walked up with a big smile and gave his comrade their secret hand shake.

"Yo Sun you! Look at the way my nigga shinning!" Referring to Ra's diamond Rolex chain, fat diamond ring, and nice tag watch.

"Yo Sun, you know that we had to up grade our game to the major league, ain't no since in fronting like we're doing bad.......fuck it kid, we're ballin Sun." Baby Tank, Little G-nut, and Juice all walked up smiling, cause they was wearing a nice diamond piece with fly gear on.

They all gave Fifty the secret hand shake and Juice said, "Yo Fifty, it's off the chain out here now! We got the whole damn projects on lock, and either niggas is working for us, or they're starving around here Sun! We had to hire look outs to keep Five-O from trying to creep Sun. And peep, we already move like four birds rock for rock! The niggas who work for us get paid on a salary basis Sun, we give them $500 dollars a day for 12 hours worth of work for us, and we got two that work on the grave yard shift, and two that work on the day shift. We give it to them for $1,200 hundred an ounce, so they still make a $300 hundred dollar profit off every ounce and this spot is going to move 18 ounces a day at the least Sun! So who can ask for more?" Juice said as he put Fifty up on their new strategy.

"I'm proud of ya'll, it seem like ya'll put it down right, fair, and very professional too." Fifty stated as they all smiled.

"Yo, that ain't all Sun, we cut you in on a bigger profit too – since you were the one who really laid the foundation to this, and made it all possible, we decided to cut you in for a extra hundred dollars off every ounce, so you're getting your $45,000 thousand dollars that we agreed upon, for the two and a half keys that you got invested, plus you get and extra $4,500 hundred dollars off every key time twelve keys that's $54,000 thousand dollars extra that we're going to cut you in for." Baby Tank said, as he did the math.

"Yo Sun, I'm honored to have such thorough and real young gorillas in my life, ya'll are the truth!"

"Naw Sun, you're the truth – we just learn from the best." Little G-nut stated.

"So who's rides are they?" Fifty gestured toward the new whips.

"OH, you like them Huh – well, the burgundy Cadillac Escalade is Little G-nut's." Little G-nut grinned as Fifty smiled at him. "And the off white Escalade is Ra's," and Ra bounced his head with a grin as everyone laughed at his gesture. "And the off white Navigator is Baby Tanks!"

"Yo, you know that I had to keep it gangsta' with the 20 inch gold D's! Baby Tank said as Ra gave him dap and everyone laughed.

"And the 500 Benz Coup is me." Juice said proudly. Everyone started laughing at him as he popped his shirt.

"O'kay now, I see my little Rades is stunting hard around this muthafucka! I'm glad to see ya'll doing good and getting money, and I don't ever want to see ya'll doing bad again. It's too many sucka's in this game for a real nigga to be starving. Feel me Sun!"

"Hell ya, I feel you!" Baby Tank said.

"And whatever you do, don't allow this little gain and glory rock you to sleep, cause it's another nigga out there waiting for you to slip, so they can come-up off you, or knock you out the way. So stay focused, loyal, and down for each-other, and we will always stay ballin and strong in the game." Fifty looked into his comrades eyes and knew that they understood him.

"Cool we got you Rade," Little G-nut said, "But listen Sun, we recruited some little gorillas, and we want to introduce them to you."

"Is that right, where are they?" Fifty asked as Little G-nut whistled and three young niggas ran up looking about fifteen to sixteen years old.

"Yo Rade, this Baby-G and Trouble, who I recruited as my little Rades, and this YG, Baby Tank little Rade. Yo Sun, say what's up to your big OG comrade Fifty! This is one of the founders and originators of the Gorillas."

Fifty smiled at his introduction and said, "Yo, what's up young comrades, it's a pleasure to meet ya'll, and I hope that our bound will grow stronger by the test of time, because in becoming apart of this Gorilla Crew, you must prove your loyalty, thoroughness, and strength, because we ride against all odds and we don't believe in weakness. So understand your commitment to this family, and represent it to the fullest." Fifty said as he stared hard into each one of their young hungry eyes and didn't detect one trace of fear or weakness. Then Fifty hit them all off with the secret hand shake and they knew it well.

"O'kay ya'll go and get that money!" Little G-nut said.

"O'kay nut, Yo Fifty it was a pleasure Sun!" The tallest one that stood six feet, two inches said as the other two said, "later Rade," and rushed off to go serve some smokers that was waiting at a distance.

"I don't know about ya'll, but I'm starving, let's go get a plate from Big Michelle and go to the apartment and chill." Ra said.

"Yo we can go hit a restaurant if you want too." Fifty said.

"Are you kidding! Yo, we give Big Michelle $500 hundred dollars a week to buy some food and cook us and our workers breakfast, lunch, and dinner, and we pay her $250 hundreds a week for her services. And believe me Sun, this big bitch is the truth! We're thinking about opening up a soul food restaurant and letting her be our cook, because she's that good!" Ra said with a serious look on his face.

"That sounds like a good investment opportunity, and it's always good to invest in something legitimate to account for your money, because if you just keep it all in a safe in your closet, you might come up short." Fifty said as they all started rolling at his inside joke.

* * * *

Summer and Tee-Tee went to a nice upper class restaurant by Manhattan Beach and was approached by a dozen men as they flirted and handed out their business cards to their escort service, and it was obvious that every man who approached them had intentions on calling real soon.

When they left, they went and walked through the Green Acres Mall and flirted with all of the older men that were shopping by themselves. They were breaking men's necks everywhere they went, and they were loving the fun and attention as they played certain games to see if they could entice certain men with different methods of seduction, and both was considered professional seductresses.

* * * *

Fifty was in the spot full and kicking it with his young comrades when his cell phone rung. He picked it up and answered it, and a familiar voice said, "What's up Rade, I finally caught up with you huh!"

"Yo Sun, what's up Rade, what took you so long to call me – Yo, Ra cut the music down abit, it's our comrade Yayo! O'kay, what's up Sun, did you get the money, and the attorney hook-up that I gave your mom?"

"Yeah bro, and that was love – word is bond G! And thanks for looking out for my Mom and sister, man I don't know how to thank you for the love and realness."

"Come on Rade, you know how we get down, your family is my family too, and when you get cut, I bleed as well. So don't trip the sentiments we're bonded for life! Yo tell me, did ya'll get that money that I sent to all of ya'll?"

Hell yeah, and your Rades in here love you to death for the loyalty and devotion you've shown them. Even Big Caesar said that he sends his love, and profound respect to you for keeping it one hundred percent with him. He said something about a big ass diamond ring that you gave to his wife and said that it was from him. That was as real as it gets. Everybody's grateful to you for the love Rade, and it's only right that you should know that we got five more Rades who just came home."

"Is that right, well our family is getting bigger by the week, because you got some thorough young comrades here that Juice and them brung home that's as real as it gets" (and the youngsters was smiling and proud of the compliment that Fifty gave them), "one is named Ra, then you got Baby Tank, and Little G-nut. I gave them all their L's (meaning lieutenant positions), and they already brung home some promising prospects."

"That's good, give them our love and respect, and tell them that we said to keep it G! And send us some pictures of them."

"Cool! Give us the new Rades name and numbers, so we can send them some paper to keep them from wanting."

"O'kay get a paper!"

Fifty got a pen and a piece of paper and wrote down his new comrades information.

"O'kay, are ya'll cool?"

"Yeah we cool, but peep! Mom's came to see me last weekend, and I gave her a message for you, from me."

"O'kay, I'll go get it tonight!"

"Okay good, and check it out! Power's mom is financially fucked up, and about to get evicted out of her spot, and he wanted to know if you can help her out, you know that she got his seed, and it's getting real hard for her!"

"Yo, say no more Sun, what's her 411....?"

And Yayo gave Fifty the hook up.

"Yo, tell him that I'm on it right now Sun – don't trip I got ya'll, and I'm about to stop by Mamma Ya's house and get that too!"

"Alright try to put that in effect for me o'kay?"

"I got you – don't trip."

"Hey – G love Rade!"

"G-love little bruh, call me back when-ever, and I'm send you some pictures of my new spot, and my ladies. You know that I got an escort services!

"Yo you're bullshiting Sun!"

"Ha, ha, ha," Fifty laughed and said, "How are you going to question me when you know my pedigree – you know that I'm the rawest nigga that you know, and when you get these pictures then you'll know for sure! Big head Ha, ha, ha!" Fifty said as he shared a good laugh with his childhood friend and god brother, and then they hung up.

"Yo Juice, these are our new comrades who just came home and was in the pen with Yayo and them, I need you to go to the post office and send them all $500 hundred dollars a piece, and let's put together a G-bank for our comrades in the pen, so we can make sure that they're able to eat good and get the things that they need. Also, see if you can find a couple of reliable people to hold it and send off the money, books, and magazine, and we'll allow them to take a hundred dollars a piece a month from it, for themselves.

"Got you Rade!" Juice said.

"Baby Tank, go to the store and by a couple of them instant cameras and take some photos of the comrade out here, for the comrade in there. And get some of these cute young bitches around here to set it out in G-strings and shit for the homies.

"I'm on it Rade!"

"Yo, I got to go handle some business for our comrades, so I'll catch up with ya'll later!"

"Alright Rade," the youngsters said as they all gave him the secret hand shake before he left.

* * * *

Fifty stopped at Mamma Ya's house and she was happy to see him. They talked for twenty minutes and she gave him a letter that was rolled up real small on a piece of paper.

Fifty unwrapped it and read it....... And it said, "Yo Rade, that bitch C/O Lynn is trying to go, she said whatever you give her, she'll bring it to us if you give her $500 dollars to do it. She said that she is gamed for whatever, and is waiting for you to contact her – here's her number. See what you can do! G-Love!"

Natural Born Gangster

Fifty smiled and kissed Mamma Ya on the cheek and left. He called C/O Lynn and she told him to stop by, Fifty use to always flirt with her, but all she did was tease him and told him maybe one day.

She was a thick dark brown skin sista' that was pleasantly plumped, and looked good in her uniform.

Fifty went over by the Baisley Projects and brought two ounces of tar heroin, and two ounces of that good grain hydro weed, that was $600 dollars an ounce. He ran to the liquor store and brought some saran wrap and a six pack of magnums condoms to tie the dope up in. He carefully wrapped it up with his gloves on, and compressed it together real small, and then placed it into two separate condoms wrapped up, so they both could fit in c/o Lynn's pussy, and be transported into the prison with no problem.

Fifty pulled up and knocked on her door, and she answered it in a low cut red silk robe. Fifty smiled at the thought knowing what was on this bitch's mind.

"Come in baby, I've been thinking about you!" C/O Lynn said.

"Is that right, well it's been many of nights I thought of you too, but it seemed like you didn't have no play for a brother!" Fifty uttered as she held him by the hand and lead him to the couch.

"Baby don't be mad at me, I just couldn't show my true feelings then, because too many people was all up in my business, and we didn't have the opportunity to enjoy it then. I worked the wrong shift to try to take that kind of chance. Would you forgive me? I want to make it up to you if possible."

"Yo peep Ma, are you going to look out for my comrades or what?"

"Of course baby, I gave my word, and I always stand on my word. Your comrade's is some thorough niggas, and I know that they won't expose my hand. So I don't mind being down with ya'll, as long as you treat me right. You don't have to kick-it with me if you don't want to, I just remember that you always told me that as soon as I give you the chance, then you was going to make me love you! I guess that-that was just all prison talk huh?"

Fifty knew that she just put him in a catch 22, and knew that if he didn't give her no dick, then she might leave his comrades hanging, but if he did, then he'll have her locked in – especially if he should take another fall, and end-up back in the prison where she works at. Fifty smiled and said, "I'm mad that you neglected me while I was down, and needed a down and real woman by my side, however I'll forgive you this time but you better not ever neglect me like that again – you hear me?"

"Yes baby - I hear you!"

"Now take off that robe and let me see what you're hiding under it, damn baby, you got that sexy thickness about your-self Ma – come and give me some of that bomb head that I use to dream about so much." And she unbuttoned his jeans and tried to suck the life up out of him. He looked down at her hard at work, and knew that she would certainly become handy.

Fifty put it down for the home team and left C/O Robin Lynn breathless and completely satisfied. Then he gave her $1000 dollars to lock her all the way in and left her wore out and feeling good. She wasn't as fine as his ladies by a long shot, but she had some bom pussy and knew how to fuck and suck, Fifty gave her a big passionate kiss and then smiled, and walked out the door.

It was 8:30p.m. when Fifty arrived at Power's mother house. He knocked on the door and an old heavy set woman answered it.

"Hello Maam, I'm looking for Mrs. Jones."

"That would be me sir!"

"Hi Maam, my name is Fifty and I'm a very good close friend of your son Eddie, he wanted to send his love to you and let you know that he will always be down with you, and there for you through your complicated struggles and hard times, and he asked me to bring you this," and Fifty handed her a envelope with $5,000 thousand dollars in it. And looked in back of her, and seen a ten year old boy that looked just like Power and Fifty smiled at them and said, "You take care and have a nice day Maam," and turned and walked away, with a smile on his face because he knew that she was totally in shock.

Chapter 14
Take Money

It was the following night and Fifty was on a cold mission as he pulled down the street from the big brick house where Fat Tony live at. Fifty got out of the car and crept up and around to the side of Fat Tony's house and looked through the window one at a time, trying to catch a glimpse and see if anyone was home, he looked though the back bedroom window and seen Fat Tony getting his freak on, as the cute black curly hair Italian bitch rode him like a cow-girl in heat. Fifty went to the back door and popped it open with the crow bar, and hope he didn't make to much noise as he grabbed his big desert eagle, and crept to the back bedroom. He heard Cash Money song playing as the Hot Boys song "Back That Ass Up" echoed through the room.

Fifty glanced into the bedroom through the cracked door, and then walked in with gun in hand as Fat Tony's eyes lit up when he seen the black man with a ski mask on. The girl was still riding him with her eyes closed when she felt Fat Tony's dick get soft in her, and she opened up her eyes to the shocking surprise of a big black gun pointed at her lover.

"Bitch, you need to slowly ease off of him and go lay your ass face down over there on the floor, and if you try anything stupid, then I'ma blow your got damn brains out all over that wall."

"Please don't shoot me – I won't do nothin' stupid." The woman said as she got up and went to lay on the floor like Fifty asked her.

"What do you want?" Fat Tony asked.

"I want you to slowly get your fat ass up, and come lay down next to her on the floor, and if you try something stupid, then I guarantee you, it will be your last!" Fat

Tony got up and did what he was told. Fifty pulled out his plastic hand restraints and place them on Fat Tony's wrist, but made sure that he placed it above Fat Tony's diamond Povade Platinum Rolex watch, and fat diamond bracelet, as Fifty took off Fat Tony's jewelry and made sure that the restraints was on tight. Then he walked over and placed some plastic restraints on the women too. "Now fat boy, you can live through this or not, that's totally up to you, all I want is the money and the dope, and you can live to fuck another day." Fifty said as he laughed at his own joke.

"I don't know what you're talking about!" Fat Tony said and Fifty slapped him across the head with the big desert eagle bustin his head on impact and Fat Tony said, "Wait a minute – I was just playing, It's in the safe in the closet, the combination is 7-2-11…!"

Fifty went to open up the safe and it was filled-up with stacks of money. "Yo, fat boy, how much money is this?"

"Around $700,000 thousand dollars!"

"Damn, you're ballin for real huh! Yo, where is the dope at?"

"I ain't got no dope in here!" Fat Tony said as Fifty walked out of the closet with a big wooden baseball bat and hit Fat Tony twice hard in the back and Fat Tony said, "Alright, alright, it's in the duffle bag in the hall closet on the floor."

Fifty went to retrieve the bag, and when he came back in the room Fat Tony was tussling trying to get loose, and Fifty kicked him hard in the nuts and curled him up in pain as his teeth gritted through the agony.

"You think that I'm playing with you? Don't make me kill your fat ass in here tonight!" The women was crying as Fifty said, "Shut the fuck up bitch before I slap you with this damn bat too!" And she shut up quick. Fifty opened up the duffle bag and seen 15 keys and smiled as he went and loaded all the money in a big suit case, and found a proper Tec 9 and a 44 magnum with a long 12 inch barrel, and packed it all up then tied both of their legs up and said, "Today's your lucky day, because I won't kill you, but you better quit trusting your friends, because they're jealous of you!"

"Who is it? Just tell me and I'll kill them, and you can keep their cut of the money too!"

"Sounds temping, but just like they asked me not to kill you, they also asked me not to cross them, so I gave my word, but I'm sure you will be able to tell real soon." And Fifty smiled as he walked out, because he knew that he just planted the seed of deception, and Fat Tony might end up killing a couple of his associates on suspicion.

Fifty went to his town house and counted the money and it came up to $735,000 thousand dollars, and he also had got 15 kilos of powder cocaine, so it was a real good lick to say the least. Fifty put the money and dope up, and changed clothes and headed back to his mansion. So he could relax and enjoy the benefits of ballin.

* * * *

The next morning Fifty woke up looking into the beautiful face of his Summer breeze, she was so naturally attractive with brains and a body that could stimulate every part of a man's desire, but a heart that could love you or despise you with the same intensity, that would make a man or break a man. To have a woman's mind and body was one thing, but to steal her soul was the ultimate task, and Fifty had to make sure that it was done effectively. Men had dogged her, used her, and abused her, all her life so only the compassion of a real man's appreciation for her should be the key to the door that was left unopened.

Fifty smiled and rolled over as Tee-Tee automatically wiggled her body backwards to cuddle up against Fifty's body for comfort. Fifty thought that she was awoke until he heard her light slumber. He smiled as he enjoyed the warmth of her full figure body pressed up against his. He knew that he possessed her soul now, and she would be devoted to him for life, and this pleased him, because trust and loyalty was everything in a relationship, and if both do not fully exist, then the long term effect could be deadly.

Fifty knew that he could settle down with both of these two beautiful and sexy ladies and be satisfied sexually and emotionally; more then 95% of the men in this world would be, but mentally he knew that he would be breaking the rules to the game, because you should never try to rehabilitate a hoe, cause just like a dope fiend, there will always be those withdrawals!

Always let a hoe play her position and play tricks, if not, then you would become her biggest trick – it's in her nature, and she's devoted to her addictions. So Fifty knew that the game had to go on, and he would forever be known to them as their man aka, Pimp!

He had a position in life too, and had to play his part to the fullest, or the game lord would probably punish him for disrespecting the game.

Fifty contemplated his next move, and smiled at the thought of hitting Fat Tony for the $700,000 hundred thousand dollars. Fifty was very close to a ticket strong, and ain't been out of prison for a whole month yet.

Oh how sweet it is, he thought as his dick was rock hard pressed against Tee-Tee fat ass, and Fifty reached around and caressed her bare breast, and Tee-Tee moaned and automatically reached back and put Fifty's dick into her wet hot pussy, and started rotating her hips, grinding to the rhythm of their heart beat. Fifty gave a scandalous grin as he pulled out of her, and rolled her over onto her back, and slid on top of her as their lustful desires caressed in total bliss.

After they ate breakfast Fifty told his ladies to get dress so he could take them somewhere special. They smiled with excitement as they rushed to get themselves dress to impress, so they could look fly as they spend the day with their man. They jumped in the Range Rover bumpin as Fifty headed to his destination. And twenty minutes later, fifty pulled up at his old friend Mocho exotic car dealership.

"Yo Ma listen up, I'ma put a down payment for whatever you want, but you will have to maintain your own payments and insurance. And with the money that you both will be making – I'm sure that you can afford to ride in style. So whatever you desire, go and get! I got you Ma!" And the ladies started screaming like little girls and jumpin on him kissing him all over his face.

"O'kay, O'kay now go!"

Tee-Tee and Summer was out of the truck and on a mission.

Mocho walked up as Summer, Tee-Tee, and Fifty was getting out of the truck and said, "Damn Poppy, you didn't tell me that your girls looked so beautiful – I want to buy some of that shit Poppy!"

"OH you like what you see huh?"

"You muthafuckin' right Poppy, they got everything, every–fuckin-thing Poppy! How much?"

"My ladies charge $500 hundred dollars for the first hour, and $250 dollars for every-other hour after that!" Fifty said firmly.

"Good Poppy, I want both for 3 hours each, tonight! You hook me up?"

"I got you!"

"Tonight at 9:00 o'clock!" Mocho stated.

"You got it my friend – now peep, I'ma put the down payment for them, and they're going to keep the payments up, you can put it in their names, and they work at my escort service so they got good employment, and as you see, they also got good liability insurance, so they can handle whatever payment that you give them."

"You damn right Poppy, they should be fuckin rich with bodies like that! Shit I pay no problem!" Mocho said with a lustful grin in his eyes.

Fifty understood, because Summer and Tee-Tee had that kind of effect on every man, so a pure sucka didn't have a chance.

"Daddy," Summer said as her and Tee-Tee came walking up to where Fifty and Mocho was standing. "We both want the brand New Cadillac Escalade trucks."

"That's a nice choice! This is my old friend Mocho, he owns this dealership and is going to hook ya'll up – also, he wants to enjoy ya'll company tonight, so he asked to reserve the 9 o'clock slot for three hours."

"Are you sure that you can handle both of us Poppy?" Summer said with a seductive smile.

"If not, I'll enjoy trying!" And everyone laughed.

"O'kay listen baby, go pick out the one's that you want, and go take it for a test drive to make sure that that's what you really want, then let's get this paperwork done."

"O'kay daddy," said Summer as both ladies walked off with their fat asses switchin' exotically.

"Damn Poppy, you're gonna' be fuckin' rich." Mocho said as he stared hypnotically at both of the ladies asses as they walked away.

Fifty laughed, and said "listen, how much down payment would I have to put down for both the trucks?"

"Listen Pappy, you give me $5,000 thousand dollars a piece, and I'll make their payments $550 dollar each! O'kay Pappy, little down payment – big monthly payment! That way, I work with you, let the bitches pay for the trucks...... Right Poppy?"

"You damn right, and I'm glad that you got a lot of game about yourself!" And Fifty gave Mocho daps, as they laughed and walked into Mocho plushed office.

Tee-Tee chose a burgundy one with cream leather seats, and Summer chose a black one with dark gray leather seats. Fifty paid the down payment and the deal was signed, sealed, and agreed upon.

They caravanned to the Red Lobster and enjoyed a nice lunch, as Fifty let them both bask in their joy for a moment as he contemplated his next move. He knew that he had to put the finishing touches on his game plan, in order to get the appropriate out come that he desired. He looked across the table at both of his ladies as they laughed and joked with each other, and Fifty said in a serious tone, "listen Ma, the stage is set, now it's time for me to see your performance.

Now peep, it's time for ya'll to recruit me some down and thorough bitches. Every woman that you recruit must be willing to come home and except her position in my life, as my lady. If she ain't no seasoned hoe, then I don't want her, because I want women that I could trust and know is down for me first, and the cause as well.

Now every lady that you bring home will receive medical and dental that we will provide though our insurance policy, plus, we will clothe them, and provide them with a room in our home, and they will make a third of their weekly income.

So, if one of our ladies makes $3,000 thousand dollars a week, then she will receive a check for $1,000 thousand dollars at the end of the week. Since you both are my bottom ladies, then I'ma provide you both with 10% of the weekly profit that you both will split aside from the third that you would make from dealing with your clients.

This will be your added profit for managing the business, so say at the end of the week, the business profit is $16,000 thousand dollars after you ladies get paid for your one third percent, and then you two would receive and extra $1,600 hundred dollars that you two would split. Do you both understand?

Both the ladies shook their heads yes!

"O'kay now, you both got some recruiting to do and some clients to find and break."

"Also, find a good doctor for our girls, because they will have to get regular check ups. You both wanted this position, and promised me that you will build me a stable of down and beautiful woman that's devoted hustlers, and thus far, I haven't' seen nothing. Your cell phone haven't rung once while we been out today, and that disappoints me, and make me question your loyalty and devotion to me and our cause."

"Baby–we-!"

"Hush! No need for words or excuses, because only your actions can show me what ya'll are about." Fifty dug in his pocket and peeled off three $50 dollar bills, and got up and said, "I'll see ya'll later," and turned and walked away without looking back or breaking his stride. He jumped in his Range Rover truck and said, "Checkmate," as he laughed and pulled off bumpin Jay-Z, hard knock life.

* * * *

It was 3:30p.m. when Fifty pulled up in-front of Nana's apartment complex, and Nina was standing out front looking as fine as ever, as she had on a one piece tight fitting Fila tennis mini-skirt out fit, and some white stiletto high heel boots. Fifty ain't called her in a week and she was up-set that he ignored her like that, but as soon as he called, she was excited and ready to kick it with him again, because she loved his swag…. And knew that he had money!

She jumped into his truck and said, "Hi Poppy! I missed you – why you haven't called me?" And she lend over and gave him a seductive kiss.

"My bad Ma, I got caught up on some important business and stuff, but I ain't forgot you, that's why I'm here now – I wanted to kick it with my young sexy tender!" Fifty said as he smiled and pulled off.

Nina knew that she had to play her cards right, because Fifty wasn't the type that she can control and persuade with her looks, so she had to be patient and just let him show her what makes him tic.

Fifty pulled up in the Inn Motel and went to go get a room. Nina was surprised, but kind of offended that he was being so cheap. She didn't mind having sex with him, if that's what he wanted, but she wished that he showed her a little more class and went to a better more expensive motel. Fifty got back in with the motel key and went to go park. Then grabbed the brown paper bag that he had the stuff that he brought from the liquor store, and a black duffle bag that Nina assumed had an extra change of clothes in it. They entered the low budget motel and it was clean, so that was a plus Nina thought!

Fifty sat the brown paper bag down and the duffle bag, and went to cut on the music from the old TV and Cash Money Bling, Bling was bumpin on the station. "Yo Ma, get naked for me, I want to see you dance in the nude!"

"What? Are you serious?" Nina asked surprised at his request.

"Of course I'm serious, unless you have a problem with satisfying your man's desires." Fifty said as he pulled out a bottle of Hennessy from the bag, and two cups and started filling the cups up as he looked at Nina and asked, "Do you want some cranberry juice mixed with yours?"

"Yeah but just a little!"

Fifty sat in the chair and sipped his drink and said, "Well Ma, what's up?"

Nina smiled and started slowly dancing to the beat and taking off her clothes like she was so used of doing. She got down to her G-string panties and her nice size titties stood straight up at attention, Fifty said to her "Those too!" And gesture toward her G-string panties and she walked over to him and said, "You pull them down for me!"

Fifty smiled as he pulled them down her legs, and seen just a small patch of hair neatly trimmed laying on top of a sexy golden bald pussy. She danced in front of him and he slowly caressed her sexy curves and realized that she had his dick on rock hard.

"You want me to leave on my boots Poppy?" She asked him in a sexy seductive voice as Fifty shook his head yes and smiled.

Fifty stood up and pulled out his dick and said, "suck it for me Ma, I want to feel your sexy lips and tongue kissing this dick, show me how much you want to be down with me," and she sat on the bed and pulled him over to her and started giving him what he asked for, and Fifty said, to himself – damn she's good!

Fifty let her suck him for about 3 minutes and pulled away, and said "I got to have some of that bomb pussy you got Ma, hold up!"

Then he got undressed as she watched him, while taking off her boots and crawled up on the bed.

Fifty reached into the bag and pulled out a magnum, and put one on his dick as he crawled up between her sexy golden body, and slip deep off into her hot wet pussy in one stroke. She cried out a painful moan as he hit her bottom, and he left his dick buried deep into her tight pussy allowing her to adjust to him while their lips and tongue seductively danced, and then he started humping long and deep as she moaned out in pleasure and started talking nasty to him in Spanish as she wrapped her legs around his body, he power drove her with deep long strokes, then he put her legs on his shoulders and really started pounding her wet tight pussy and she was loving every minute of it, as she felt her first orgasm hit, he felt her pussy tighten up around his dick and he slowed down his pace, and started stroking her with long slow deep strokes, when her eyes opened back up, he kissed her and told her to get in a doggie position.

He got behind her and ran two fingers between her pussy lips, stealing the wetness from it, then slid his dick back in from the back and started pounding it in and out, as she rammed her butt back to meet his every thrust. Fifty took his finger and slid it up in her tight ass hole, and her pussy tighten up as her second orgasm arrived sending him over board with her as their bodies tightened up and shook in ecstasy. Nina cried out in pleasure then said, "OH Poppy, you make me cum so good!"

They both layed on the bed breathing hard, and then they both started laughing.

"Damn Poppy, you got that bomb dick!"

"You got it real good too Ma!" Fifty said as he rubbed her fat butt and got up and went to flush his condom and wash off his dick, and when he came back and handed her a hot wet towel. Then he went over to the big black duffle bag and unzipped it, and poured the money all over the bed and Nina', eyes got big with a surprised look, then she looked up at Fifty, and Fifty said, "that's yours Ma! Compliments of Fat Tony!"

"You're kidding – Oooowow baby, you got that fat muthafucka?" Fifty shook his head. How much is it Poppy?"

"Well I had to take a couple of my comrades to help me, so after splitting it four ways, you made out with $125,000 thousand dollars!"

"Oooowow Pappy, that's a lot of money – I ain't never seen this much money before in my life!"

"Well that's what happens when you fuck with the real…. Real thangs happen! But I'll advise you to sit on it for a minute before you start spending it on any and everything, because you don't want to draw no unwanted attention to yourself, and get our self caught up about it. Feel Me?"

"Yes I feel you Poppy."

So tell me, what are you going to do, are you trying to work for my escort service or what?" Fifty asked knowing that now that she got all that money, that he'll probably never see her again.

"Oh yeah Poppy – I want to still work for you, and be down for you, but I just got to take care of a couple of things first O'kay?"

"Sure Ma, I feel ya!" Said Fifty knowing that she didn't have the truth in her." Yo ma, put that back in the bag and lets go jump in the shower, so I can hit that bomb pussy again before we leave."

"O'kay Poppy."

They jumped in the shower and Fifty hit her in all three of her sexy holes, then dropped her ass off and laughed, knowing that he probably wouldn't see her again.

* * * *

Fifty got a call from Ra saying that they needed them four birds, so Fifty went and jumped into his Cadillac Seville rent-a-car, and took them the work.

As Fifty pulled up the youngsters was waiting for him and they followed him into the house. Fifty was a master chef so he cooked the dope up for them, and was finished in no time. "Ya Fifty, I got to go pick up my little comrades from around the way, why don't you ride with me and kick it with your Rade for a minute," Little G-nut said.

"Cool Rade, I'll roll with you!"

"Yo, let's ride then Sun!"

"Hold up ya'll, I'm coming too!" Baby Tank said, as they all jumped in Little G-nut's Escalade truck and rolled out. Little G-nut had 18 inch woofers in the back, and they were pounding the bass from Little Wayne's new cut the 'Block is Hot'!"

"Damn that little niggas hard Sun!" Baby Tank said referring to Little Wayne's lyrics.

"He's right!" Fifty said as they pulled up to a music studio on Jamaica Ave.

"What's here?" Fifty asked as they got out of the truck.

"Oh, this is a new recording studio that they just built over here, my little comrade be trying to put their game on tape so they can try to blow up." Little G-nut stated as they entered the studio.

"Are they any good?" Fifty asked.

"Yeah their game is real tight!" Little G-nut said proudly as they entered the rehearsing studio that they were in.

"Yo, that's Jay!" Fifty said as he seen one of his favorite old school producers.

"Yeah I gave Baby-G and them some extra change, so they can get a good beat from him."

"That's love! And they sound like they got a little talent!"

"A little? Sun, they got mad skills! Ain't that right Baby Tank?

"Yeah, I like them!"

"Man come on Sun, they're alright – they still got titties in their mouth – spitting that old school Big Daddy Kane, Heavy D shit. That shit was lost in the 80's, they need to get with that new style, that gangsta, ghetto shit. They got the right beat, but the wrong lyrics."

Fifty said as him and Baby Tank started laughing.

"Yo Sun, do you think that you can do better?" Little G-nut asked in a hostile tone?

"Sun, I'll crush them little niggas!"

"Oh yeah, Oh yeah, hold up ya'll, cut, cut! And the music went off as Trouble, Baby G and Y.G. all existed the booth."

"What's up Sun?" Y.G. asked.

"Ya'll hold up – Jay my Rade is gong to try his hand, he think that he can fuck with my young Rades. Go ahead – let us hear what you got."

"You must not know who I am!" Fifty uttered and said, "Yo Jay, slow that beat down for me a bit, and bring up that bass a tad bit."

Jay said, "You got it Sun!" And Fifty went into the booth.

"Yo, I want ya'll to murder his ass when he finish – I mean dog him out Sun!"

"Got you Little G-nut!" Trouble said.

Fifty put on the headphones and road the beat for a second and said, "You know what happens when you put a puppy in the cage with a full blooded, full grown killa pitbull? They call it puppy chow!" Fifty laughed as two dudes and two cute ladies was walking into the studio to ear hustle. Fifty said, "Do we have any Fakster's in the room? Yeah, I see a couple," and the beat dropped again and Fifty started spitting his rap about them broke ass niggas who be fronting but don't have nothing.

The girl that walked in with the two guys and her girlfriend, looked over at her girlfriend and said, "Oooowow girl, he got mad flow!"

And Little G-nut looked over at the girl dancing to the beat, and then Baby Tank said, "Yo Sun, that nigga's the truth B!" And Y.G. shook his head in agreement.

When Fifty stopped, Little G-nut said, "Drop a different track on him," and Jay did it and Fifty put down a rap about jackin a star, and the studio went wild as they listened to Fifty drop some mad jewels.

The song went off and Fifty said, "Is that all you got Jay?" Then Jay dropped him a different beat. And Fifty seen the girls jockin and he said, "Yo Ma, are you down!" And he pointed at the girls and they smiled and shook their heads, and Fifty did his song called 'Questions'! He was asking the girls would they be down through the hard times, and they was loving his style and flow as well as everyone else. The guys that they came in with seen their ladies jockin and said, "Come on, let's go!"

As the ladies was walking out Fifty said, "You and your friend, I hope I see you both again!" Then the youngsters and Jay started rolling.

Little G-nut looked over at Trouble and Baby-G and said, "Ya'll better stand down Rades, he's strapped pretty good!"

Baby G said, "I wasn't going to jump out there – Sun's a monster!"

"Yeah, the big homie got man lyrics Sun." Trouble stated and gave Y.G. dap.

Fifty came out of the booth and everyone gave him dap! "Yo Sun, you set that shit ablaze! I didn't know that you was vicious like that!"

"Man – I held down the yard at Clinton, for the three years that I was there! I was just clowning then, I didn't even pull out the big guns yet Sun!"

"Yo Fifty peep, here's a copy of your lyrics on tape for you, I got another copy over there, that I would like to put one of your songs on this mix CD that I'm putting together – it's strictly promotional, but if it get a good buzz, then the radio stations would push it, and you might can come up with a good record deal."

"Yo, you think so?"

"It's no harm in trying, but you got to give me verbal permission to put it on my mix tape for promotional purposes only. That means even if my mix tapes do blow up, then all you got was free promotion, and your music out in the streets.

"Fuck it, handle your business Sun, you got my permission!'

"I appreciate it, and truth be told, I worked with a lot of big artistes in this music industry, and very few can deliver lyrics like you. You got a good gift, and I hope that this will help you take it to the next level."

"I hope so too – and I appreciate your assistance Jay, much love Sun!"

Chapter 15
Got To Love A Boss Player

Fifty spent the next three days kicking it and spending time with his Grandma and Grandpa. He took them both shopping for new clothes the first day, and out to dinner at a fancy Five Star restaurant. The next day he took them to the Museum of natural history in Manhattan, because he knew that they had never been there. The third day he took them to see Chris Tucker get his clown on at the Apollo Theater, and he never seen his Grandmother and Grandfather laugh so hard in his life, that alone made his day with them seem so special. After the Apollo, he took them to a nice Jazz Club, and let them dance the night away like when they were younger, and it was a beautiful sight to see. He dropped them off and gave them a big legal envelope with $15,000 thousand dollars and two all expense paid tickets to Hawaii, and just the warmth of their smiles made his heart skip a beat. He gave them both a big hug and kiss on the cheek and left.

* * * *

Nina pulled up at the strip club that she use to work at, in her new blue 1998 600 Benz Coup sitting on 20" inch chrome Lorenzo's, and all attention was on her as she stepped out in a all white $2,600 hundred dollar leather Donna Karen suit, with some all white ill skin boots to compliment the two piece outfit. She seen Cream standing out front of the club with some tight sexy shorts on, with ass hangin' out the back every where.

"Hi Nina," Cream said, as Nina just looked at her like she wasn't shit, and rolled her eyes in the $1,200 hundred dollars Versace shades, and walked right by her. "Oh no this little trifflin' heifer didn't, she must think that she's the shit now, because she's flossing some oh trick ass nigga whip." Cream said as she observed the fly ass Benz Coup that Nina was driving. "I seen better!" Cream said to herself as she stood outside the door smoking a cigarette.

Nina ran into the club and picked up her last week check, and when Oscar the owner asked Nina why she hasn't been in to work, Nina Said, "because I quit, you fat nasty piece of shit!" And laughed as she walked right back out.

When she got back outside Cream said, "So who's car are you driving this time?" In a sarcastic tone.

"It's mine bitch why?"

"Yeah right, like I'm supposed to believe that you own that!"

"Bitch I ain't got to lie to you look, here's the pink slip and registration! Everybody ain't running around here selling pussy and broke like you. Nina laughed as she jumped into her new Benz and turned up the $5,000 thousand dollar sound system, bumping to Big Smalls song, 'Get Money' and pulled off.

Cream was so mad, she turned a reddish complexion as she walked back into the club and jumped on the phone.

"What's up baby? Who's this?"

"It's your sexy Cream baby!"

"Yo, what do you want, I'm busy and ain't got time to talk!"

"Damn is that the way you treat me, and to think....... I was calling you to give you the information on who jacked you!"

"What, wait baby! I was just playing! You know that I'm under a lot of stress."

"Well I am too, and I need 10g's for my problems!"

"O'kay, O'kay baby, but this better be reliable!"

"OH it is, bring the money to my job and make it rain baby." Cream said as she hung up the phone and gave a scandalous grin.

* * * *

Summer and Tee-Tee was at their favorite Mexican restaurant waiting for Fifty to arrive, they called him and told him that it was important, and he said that he was on his way.

He ain't seen them, and refuse to really talk to them for three whole days and ain't been home, and Summer and Tee-Tee was going crazy trying to get things up and running. They must've both had eight dates a piece in those three days. Fifty walked in with his hand inside of his coat, as he gripped the butt of his new Gloc 9mm.

"Hi daddy," Summer said as her and Tee-Tee stood up to greet their man with a big hug and a kiss.

"We'd like to introduce you to three beautiful young ladies who's interested in coming home. We told them that only you can make that decision, and we wanted you to meet them and see if they fit your expectation.

This is Cat!" Cat stood up and greeted him with a hug. She was a gorgeous sista mix with black and Asian. She was a beautiful brownish tan complexion with long black wavy hair, and tight Asian eyes that made her look like an Egyptian.

She had a sexy petite body with big hips and ass. She was a stripper friend of Tee-Tee that worked at Dreams, the other popular strip club that Tee-Tee use to work at.

"And daddy this is Goldie!" Goldie was another one of Tee-Tee stripper friends, but Goldie left the attic and went to Dreams to dance. Goldie was a beautiful blond hair innocent looking white girl, with blue eyes and a body like a well shape sista. She reminded Fifty of those sexy big butt white girls that be in them butt man magazines.

Fifty smiled as she turned and went to sit back down." And this is Tastie!" And Tastie stood up and walked over and gave Fifty a hug and a kiss on the cheek."

What happened to her?" Fifty asked when he seen the bruise on the side of her face.

"Well daddy, Tastie use to work with me at my old job, and her man decided that he wanted to kick her ass one night, because she slept to long and missed two hours worth of work time."

Fifty gently rubbed her bruised face. And she grabbed his hand and kissed the inside of his palm. Tastie was a super cute Brazilian girl, who had shoulder length jet black curly hair, with light gray and dark blue mixed eyes, a beautiful tan mocha complexion, with little sexy pointed titties and a nice round ass to go with her thick hips and thighs.

"Well it's a pleasure to meet you all, and it's obvious that my ladies know my taste, and the class of women that I desire in my life, because I can tell that they took pride in their selections."

Fifty looked around the table and met every ladies stare with a gentle smile. "Therefore, I'm not going to waste your time with senseless thoughts, you're obviously here because you want to be here, and you desire the love, respect, loyalty, and bond that our family embraces, as we strive together to enjoy the wealth and the gains that comes from playing these sucka's. So, we truly got a common interest and goal in life. But my question to you is; do you think that you have the real qualities that I look for in my devoted companions. Because once you come into my life, you become a part of my family, you will become my wife and spiritual soul-mates, and you all will become sisters to one another. If some one should harm one of us, then we all will feel the pain, and will plot to get revenge. I don't believe in hitting my ladies (and he looked at Tastie), because I believe that that's a weak minded sucka's way of trying to gain control, instead, I stand on my word as law, and if one of my ladies chose not to honor this, then I'll dismiss her as a bad habit, and will look else where for someone better. If you decide to disrespect my rules, then I won't hesitate to hand out a punishment that I will find equal to the violation of the rule, and if you choose not to accept it, then I will dismiss you, because your loyalty and devotion means everything and if you are lacking in one, then you will never be balance in the other.

My number one rule is always keep your man satisfied, because if I'm not satisfied, then my house could never be a home.

Second rule is being loyal to the cause and each other. I don't like a woman who bitches all the time, and jealousy is definitely forbidden.

Third rule is; get the money! I want to see all of my ladies having the best out of life, and in order for us to be able to live large; we got to hustle and keep these sucka's broke and sprung.

The fourth rule is; no hard drugs are permitted! Weed and alcohol is cool, but I don't need no dope fiend ass bitch on my team, because she would just destroy the dreams that we're chasing. So if you got a habit, then this is your chance to get rid of it, so you can have something good in your life.

Now, Summer and Tee-Tee is my two bottom ladies, that means that they will always watch over you like a big sister's, and be there for you. They run the business aspect of the escort service, and their authority is law when I'm gone, but if they should do something that you know is against our objective, then you have the right to call a meeting, and express your concerns, because we are a family, and everyone of my ladies has a voice they can share. Only my word is final on matters of dispute.

"Now do anyone have any questions?"

"Good!"

"Tastie, do you desire to be a part of this family and live by the standards that I've expressed here?"

"Yes Poppy, I want to be down with you and my sisters."

"Cat, do you desire to be a part of this family and be devoted to the standards that I've just expressed to you?"

"Yes daddy, I'm down, and want to be devoted to you and our family."

"Goldie, is this also what you want and desire too beautiful?"

"Yes daddy, I choose you, and will be down to the fullest to you and our family."

"Well, it's only right that we seal this marriage with a kiss, so everyone must kiss each other to show your devotion and love to one another!"

And everyone started kissing each other and laughing. The manager walked over and said, "excuse me Sir., I'ma have to ask you and your party to leave!" Everyone started laughing as Fifty picked up his two hundred dollar tip from off the table, and stuck it back inside his pockets, and walked out.

Summer and Tastie jumped in the Range Rover with Fifty as Tee-Tee caravanned behind them with Goldie and Cat with her.

They drove up and Tastie, Cat, and Goldie were all mesmerized by the beautiful lavish sight of the Mansion. Fifty said, "Welcome home ladies!" And they all started screaming with excitement.

Fifty opened the door and hit the alarm code and said, "You ladies have six bedrooms to choose from, so go and occupy the one you desire." The ladies all rushed up stairs full of excitement. Fifty looked at Summer and Tee-Tee and said, "I see ya'll stepped up your game a little.... I'll give you a little props."

"Well, me and Tee-Tee also made $5,000 thousand dollars while you were gone."

"OH yeah, ya'll getting money like that this early in the game! Well I guess that I got to give ya'll a little lovin' tonight then!"

"A little?" Tee-Tee said!

"I said that you two stepped your game up, not that you made it to the play off's!" And they laughed as Tee-Tee slapped him on the butt. "Now go and show your sisters around and meet me in the family room when you're done." And the ladies walked upstairs to get the girls and show them around.

Ten minutes later they all was standing up butt ass naked in front of Fifty as he walked around rubbing, caressing, and admiring his ladies beautiful structure and weaponry.

"Lovely, you all are truly a beautiful and lovely sight. I got you all a gift, this is a special gift that represents your devotion to me, and this cause that we represent.

It's an ankle bracelet, and as you can see, Tee-Tee and Summer wear theirs with a deep sense of pride and devotion, and with every step that you take, let it be for your man, and the cause that you and your sisters represent as one!"

Then Fifty took out three diamond ankle bracelets and clipped them around Goldie, Tastie, and Cats ankle.

Then he took out two fat three caret diamond bracelets and placed them around Tee-Tee and Summers' wrist, then grabbed five pairs of diamond ear rings and gave each lady a different pair.

Fifty had taken the fat Povade diamond Rolex watch that he got off of Fat Tony and took it to the jewelry store downtown, and traded it for a gang of other less expensive jewelry, and that's were he got all the jewelry from.

The ladies were riding on cloud nine, hoping that Fifty would decide to have an orgy with them. Fifty knew this as he toyed with their hot sexy bodies, then kissed everyone of them and said, Welcome home ladies!

Summer, Tee-Tee can I holler at you two for a second, ladies, make yourself at home, in your new home!" Everyone smiled at his humor.

"What's up daddy?"

"Listen, here is $13,000 dollars, take the ladies shopping and get them all $4,000 dollars worth of new clothes, then take them to the beauty salon and get them hooked up – I want Tastie to get a short wavy hair cut to show off them killer eyes."

"O'kay daddy whatever you want!"

Summer said, as they all got dressed and left. Fifty sat in his soft lazy boy chair and watch videos in his big state of the art home theater. His thoughts wondered, then dosed off with a pleasant smile on his face.

* * * *

"Yo Shorty, this better be good." Fat Tony said as he sat in the private lap dance room with Cream.

"Give me my money first!" Cream said, as she held her hand out.

"Here, but don't play with me bitch!"

Cream glanced through the money real quick.

"Bitch, I ain't gonna' cheat you for no damn crumbs"

"O'kay, o'kay, it was that scandalous ass bitch of yours Nina!"

"Nina? Bitch your crazy – she ain't stupid enough to do no shit like that, plus she didn't even know where I lived at, only you did!" And Fat Tony jumped up with the swiftness of an alley cat, and grabbed Cream by her long blond hair and said, "Bitch I think that you're trying to play me to throw me off your tracks."

"Tony – I wouldn't do no shit like that to you! And she did know where you lived at, because she followed us that day we kicked it, and seen me and you go to your house. That's why we got into it that time, she said that I took her man and when I tried to deny it, she admitted that she followed us. She's even got a brand new 600 Benz Coup sitting on 20 inch chrome rims, and with a hell-a-va sound system." Fat Tony released his grip on her hair and said, "How do you know that it was hers?"

"Because the bitch showed me the damn pink slip, flossin on me – that's how! And I heard that she fucks with this baller ass nigga out of Guy Brewer Projects name Fifty.

"Who?"

"Fifty! The nigga from that Gorilla crew!"

"I heard of him, how he look?"

"He's medium height with a nice muscular frame like a running back!"

"What do he drive?"

"Man – I don't know! I told you what I know...... now the rest is on you!"

"O'kay, but promise me that you won't tell nobody else about it!"

"Don't worry, your secret is good with me!" Cream said, as she switched out the door and her big sexy ass hung out of her butty shorts that she was wearing. Fat Tony was in a daze, as he got up and left.

Cream decided to leave early because she made a pretty good lick charging up Fat Tony's sorry ass, she thought as she laughed and walked into her two bedroom apartment. "Hey Jan – I'm home, and you wouldn't believe what happen today." Cream said, as she walked and looked in Jan's bedroom, and saw Jan laying in a puddle of blood. Cream ran over to see what happened and seen her friend throat cut. "Oh my god, Jan! What happen?"

"I don't think that she's going to tell you," a familiar voice said, as Cream tried to jump up and run when she saw Fat Tony out of the corner of her eyes. But, when she tried to jump up and run, Fat Tony swung and hit her in the head with a crow bar, and split her head wide open.

Then he stabbed her twice in the heart. "You know I can't trust you baby, you can't keep a secret." Fat Tony said, as he went and grabbed his money out of her purse and left out.

Chapter 16
Keeping It "G" 4 Life

Fifty spent two days kicking it with his ladies enjoying their character and the passion that they all devotedly gave. All of the ladies was bon-a-fide hustlers to the game, and knew all of the sucka characteristics of a man, and they were born with the weapon needed to seduce and conquer every weakness a man possessed. Fifty knew this, as he laid back by the pool and watched his ladies walk around in their G-string bathing suits, and seductively moved their hips to the beat as Hot97 the local radio station played Snoop Doggs song 'Murder Was the Case That They Gave Me'. Tastie and Cat was grooving to the beat, and Fifty was caught in a semi-hypnotized trans by their alluring act. Summer walked up behind Fifty as he laid back in the big cushion lounge chair, and grabbed his hard on through his swimming trunks and said, "Do you want me to release the pressure for you?"

Fifty looked up and smiled, and said, "No baby, this is just a training exercise; he's just stretching a bit."

They started bustin-up as Summer said, "Boy, you're crazy! And you know what?"

"What?"

"We love you so much – and I believe that I speak for all of your wives. All they do is talk about you, and how glad they are to finally found a man who's every thing they desire in a companion. They said that they rather share a real man, then to have a whole man that's a sucka'!"

Fifty felt the genuine love in her heart, as she spoke her thoughts and emotional confessions to him, and Fifty knew that deep down inside, he loved them all too, but refuse to let down his guards.

"Cat, Summer, you both got a two o'clock appointment with your judge friend Mr. Frank."

"Well I better grab the handcuffs and big paddle!" Everyone started laughing at Summers humor.

Goldie, Doctor Roberts requested a 1:30p.m. appointment from you, so you got an hour to get dress and get there.

"I'm on it sis, Goldie said as she got up naked from Sun bathing, and switched by Fifty, and stole a kiss as she walked into the house.

"Tastie your NBA friend set up a six o'clock appointment for you, and said wear your leather and bring your bag."

"Freaky ass nigga!" Fifty said as everyone started bustin-up.

Just then Fifty cell phone rung, "Yo! O'kay! I got you! I'll be there in 30 minutes. O'kay out!"

"Duty calls!" Fifty said as he kissed Summer and pulled her off his lap, and stood up and left.

Fifty had 23 keys stashed away from his previous licks, and supplied his young crew with them so they could get paid without having to use their own profits yet to re-cop, plus Fifty was getting $21,200 dollars off of each key. Fifty pulled up at the Guy Brewer Projects at 1:00p.m., and it was all business as usual. As the youngsters embraced him and followed him in the apartment to conduct their business. Fifty brung them five keys and took Baby G, Y.G. and Trouble in the kitchen and showed them how to cook up dope the professional way. After the third kilo, the youngster was like pro's as Fifty stood back and watch his young protégé's put in work.

* * * *

Nina was driving down Van Wyck Express Way, showing off her new 600 Benz Coup bumpin Tupac's 'All Eyes On Me' CD, with the woofers beatin loud when a

1996 Ford Explorer slammed on the brakes right in front of her. She was just picking-up her cell phone dialing on it, and before she could react, her 600 Benz Coup ran smack dead off in the back of the Explore truck causing the air bags to explode, as her body jerked in the seat belt and her face smashed up against the softness of the air bag.

Nina sat in shock for a couple of minutes, and tried to gain her composure. She realized that she wasn't hurt and stepped out of her car as an older black man ran up to her and said, "Maam, are you o'kay?"

"Yeah I think so," she said as she seen her new 600 Benz Coup whole front end smashed up like a soda can. She walked up to the driver side of the Ford Explore and seen two men and a woman sitting in the truck holding their neck and moaning. "Are ya'll alright?"

"Hell naw bitch we're not alright. Someone call 911! We need to exchange information too. Bring me your license and insurance card!"

"I don't have no insurance!"

"Yo, wait a minute – what bitch! What do you mean, you don't have no damn insurance?" The man said as everyone in the truck stopped moaning and acting hurt.

"I've just brought the car a couple of days ago, and I haven't had time to get it insured yet."

"You got to be kiddin, how did you get a hundred thousand dollar car with no insurance!" The lady in the front seat said. Didn't the car dealership give you full coverage when you brought it?"

"No I brought it from a private owner!"

"Hell naw kid, out of all the muthafucken people in the world, you had to pick a bitch with no damn insurance." The man in the back seat of the truck complained.

"I wonder do Chuck got insurance on this truck?" The driver asked the other two occupants.

"Hell naw man, he's a damn smoker… fuck this shit, let's roll out before 5-0 gets here! The man in the back seat said.

"Yo Shorty, even though your in the wrong, we're not going to file a complaint on you to get you fucked up, so consider yourself lucky." The driver said as he started up the truck and rolled off.

Nina looked at her car as a tear rolled down her cheak. She just paid $95,000 thousand dollars for the car of her dreams, only to loose it a couple of days later, by some niggas trying to come up. Nina went over to her car and drove it to a vacant lot, left the keys in the ignition still running, grabbed her purse and started walking, as Tupac song 'Picture Me Rollin' echoed from the sound system.

Nina walked to her sister's two bedroom old brick house and when she got there she was mad, and disgusted. She had spent $95,000 thousand dollars on her new car, $25,000 thousand dollars on her clothes and jewelry, and gave her sister $3,000 thousand dollars on GP, and after spending $1200 hundred dollars on miscellaneous shit, she only was left with $800 hundred dollars, not including the $2,000 dollars that she had saved from dancing.

She knew that she'll be straight if Fifty came through for her on that other lick, but knew that Fifty probably wouldn't even call her, if he did hit the lick, being that she lied to him about wanting to work for him.

But what if she called him and asked to be down with him, would he even accept her? It's worth a try Nina thought as she smiled and picked-up the phone.

* * * *

Fifty walked into his mansion at 7:30p.m. and was greeted by Summer, Cat, and Goldie as he said, "ladies, I like ya'll to meet your new sister, this is Nina! Nina that's Cat, that's my girl Goldie, and this is Summer, one of my bottom ladies. I'm sure that you already know Tee-Tee, she's my other bottom lady and Tastie must be out getting money, because I don't see her either, anyway you'll meet her later on tonight.

"O'kay."

"Hi Nina?" Summer said as she gave her a warm embrace and said, "Welcome home! Come on – let me help you with your things Oooowow, you got a lot of suit cases, come on I'll show you around."

"O'kay – this is nice Poppy, I didn't know that you was doing it like this!" Nina said.

"Oh, you must've thought a brotha' was faking! Ma, ain't nothing fake about me, I'm the real and uncut." And everyone started laughing.

"Let me help you too – Summer I got this one," Goldie said as she grabbed one of the big suit cases from Summer.

"Do you need me to grab one of them?" Cat asked Nina.

"Yo slow up Ma, I want to holla at you in private about something." Fifty said as he smiled seductively and grabbed her hand, "come on let's go to your room." Fifty said as everyone started making cat calls at them, as Fifty followed behind Cat up the stairs watching her fat ass dance in her little come fuck me shorts. Fifty seen her fat ass bounce up the stairs and said, "witchcraft!" as Cat lead him into her private quarters, and gave him everything that he wanted and more.

Fifty was sitting on the couch with all of his ladies butt naked kneeling down in front of him, as he laid down the laws to Nina. Nina was over whelmed at the love and acceptance, that she couldn't help but to believe in the shit that Fifty was laying down to her. She knew that Fifty had been the realest nigga in her life, and she wanted to play her position in his life now more then ever. She seen how all of his ladies was extremely beautiful and down for him and each other, and she really wanted to be a part of this new family of hers.

She received her ankle bracelet, and was turned on by the way the ladies all kissed her after she was accepted. She was always bi-sexual, and now she would be around her breed of ladies, knowing that this is where she always desired to be.

Tee-Tee said, "We got a bachelor party that requested four ladies – who wants to go?"

"I'll go sis!" Nina volunteered.

"O'kay me, Cat, Nina and Summer will go, and you two can stay here and kick it with daddy." And Tastie and Goldie smiled at the suggestion.

The next day, Fifty sent Summer to take Nina to the doctor to get checked out, and to the mall to hook her up with some fly and sexy gear. Nina loved clothes and even though she had a fat wardrobe, she still jumped at the opportunity to get some more fly gear. Fifty considered it his way of saying always keep it fly!

It was Friday afternoon and Fifty was lounging around his mansion chillin' with Tee-Tee, Cat, Goldie, and Tastie when he received a disturbing phone call.

"Hello is this Fifty?"

"Who want's to know?" Fifty asked.

"This is Fat Tony…! Do you remember me?"

"Yo, you must have me mixed up with someone else – I don't think that I know you." Fifty said as his thought was racing trying to figure out Fat Tony's angle!

"Sure you do nigga – you took something from me a while back, and I want it back!"

"Are you sure that you got the right person kid? Because I think that you got me confused with someone else."

"I seriously doubt it, because I never forget a voice! Listen, somebody want's to speak to you."

"Hi Poppy, they grabbed me and Summer at the 'Pow'!

A gun shot went off and Fat Tony said, "She had to go, but I got somebody else here who wants to say hi...!"

"Ooowow daddy, he just shot Nina in the head-!"

"Summer, Summer!"

"YOU BASTARD, you didn't have to shoot her!" Summer said in the background as he heard a loud slap and then silence.

"Yeah excuse me Fifty – you know how these bitches are."

"If you touch her again I'll kill you!" Fifty shouted into the phone.

"Listen Rico Suave, I want my money back, or I'ma kill this bitch too! Now the way that I see it, you owe me a million dollars, and you got an hour to get it together, and if you don't, then I'ma do something real big with this pretty bitch of yours, it's going to be something so horrible that the news won't even show it!"

"Hold up man – where do you want to meet at?" Fifty asked.

"Listen, meet me at the Green Acres Mall outside of the food stands in an hour, and don't be late, or you might be too late! And if I see any Pigs or any of your crew members, then I'll blow this bitch head off. Give me a mill ticket and well call it even, I already got who I wanted to get, now the next move is on you."

"I got the money and I'll be there!"

"I hope so – one hour!" (click) Fat Tony hung up as Fifty looked at his watch and then notice Tee-Tee standing next to him staring in his face.

"Baby what's going on?" Tee-Tee asked in a nervous voice.

"He kidnapped Nina and Summer – Nina's dead and he wants a mill ticket for Summer!"

"Oh shit baby, what are we gonna' do?"

"You're going to stay here and continue to watch over your sisters and run this business – I'ma go get your sister or die trying."

"Oh baby, I want to go with you!"

"No Tee-Tee! I need you to stay here and hold up our foundation to this dream, and your obligations to me and this cause, because if I get busted, then I'ma need you out here making moves for me. Don't worry; this is the way I like to play!" Fifty said with death in his eyes, and then he dialed Juice's cell phone number.

"Hello!"

"Yo Juice!"

"Yo what's up Rade I was just thinking about you."

"Yo Rade peep, I got a problem, tie the black flag – I'll be their in 30 minutes."

"Got you!"

"Out!" Fifty hung up the phone and Tee-Tee ran into his arms. "Listen Ma, I'll be back soon, but if not – then I need you to hold this down! I got to go!"

"Where are you meeting him at?"

"The mall – he wants a crowd of people around, so it might get real ugly." Fifty said as he ran and jumped into the Cadillac Seville and rushed off to his town house and grabbed $800,000 thousand dollars of his money, leaving him $150,000 thousand dollars for attorney fee's in case of an emergency.

He threw on his black leather coat and grabbed his two 45's automatics and put them in his shoulder holster, and grabbed his big Desert Eagle and put it in his waste band. Then put two extra clips for his 45 automatic in his pocket.

He threw on his dark sun glasses and black New York fitted cap, and left out the door. He made it to the Guy Brewer Projects with 25 minutes to spear, and when he walked into the apartment, all of his young Comrades was there patiently waiting.

"What's up Sun – what's the word!" Baby Tank said as he gripped his new Tec 9 with the silencer and infer red beam attached.

"Yo Rades, it's about to get real bloody and a lot of innocent people might get hurt or even killed on this mission, you might even die or end up in prison for the rest of your life if you get caught slippin, so if you don't think that your down to take that kind of chance, then you need to walk out that door now, and don't look back!" (Everybody looked around but no body left.)

"O'kay, this Italian muthafucka that I jacked a while back name Fat Tony, just kidnapped two of my ladies, he killed one already over the phone, and is threatening to kill the other one if I don't bring him this ticket.

He wants to meet at the Green Acres Mall at the food section, and I know that his crew is going to be all around, and laying in the cut.

Now once the transaction is made, it's going down, so try to be inconspicuous and low key, and watch out for the booby traps that his crew may be trying to set.

If shit gets out of hand, then get the fuck on, and if the police get at you, then shoot to kill, and try to hide your faces from the cameras, cause they can ID you too!

Let's ride – Ra! You, Baby Tank and Y.G. watch each other backs, and Little G-nut, you take Baby G, and Trouble! Juice you be my shadow.

Make a good plan, and go with it, and may the G's who rest in peace, watch our backs!"

Everyone gave each other their secret hand shake, and was out the door ready for war.

* * * *

Listen bitch! I'ma give your man five more minutes to get here, then I'ma blow your damn head off right here in front of everyone and walk out, so you better hope that he thinks you're worth a million dollars, because if not, your ass is magget food!" Fat Tony said as he held his big 357 magnum to Summer's spine, with his hand hiding in a black leather bag to conceal the truth.

Summer just knew that it was over for her, because ain't no player in the game gonna' pay a million dollars for no hoe, she ain't even made a fraction of that much money for him yet, so why should he use it to help save her, she thought as reality set in!

"Oh shit, I must've been wrong about you, you got to have some good pussy." Fat Tony said as he seen Fifty walking up with a big black sports bag around his shoulder. Summer seen Fifty walking up and her heart skipped a beat, as she let out a gentle smile of relief.

Two of Fat Tony's men stood up to stop Fifty from walking all the way up, Fifty stopped 20 feet away from where Summer and Fat Tony stood, and Fifty said, "What's up Ma, you alright?"

"I am now!" Summer said with a smile.

"Don't be so sure of that yet bitch! Yo nigger, let them have the money." Fat Tony said as his partner tried to reach for the bag and Fifty grabbed the butt of his gun and said, "Hold up! Let my lady go first!" Fifty saw Juice out of the corner of his eyes go and sit down eating a hot dog four tables away from where Fat Tony was holding Summer at.

"Listen fool, I don't have time for no fuckin' games today!"

"O'kay listen, let her walk over there by the exist, so I'll know that your not going to hurt her, and I'll give them this money." Fifty unzipped the bag so Fat Tony's men could see all the stacks of money in it.

The two men shook their heads to let Fat Tony know that it was real money, and Fat Tony said, "If you do something stupid, then I'ma kill this nigger bitch right in front of you – so try me!"

"Man you got that, you can have the damn money! Nobody needs to get hurt over this shit."

Fat Tony looked at Summer and said, "Walk your fuckin ass over there by that exist, and if you do something dumb or try to run, then I'ma kill him, then catch up with you and blow your brains out too! Now walk over there slow bitch!"

She started walking toward the open sitting court exist that was in the middle of the food court, and Fifty handed Fat Tony's partners the big black bag and as they started walking back toward Fat Tony with the bag, Fifty saw Juice grab Summer by the hand and push her behind the tile brick wall, and pulled out his Gloc as Fifty pulled his Desert Eagle out, and Fat Tony and his two partners also simultaneously grabbed for their guns, but the one with the black duffle bag that had the money was to slow, and Fifty's Desert Eagle slug hit him right in the chest and blew out his back, as the two shots ripped right threw him. The other man shot blindly as Fifty moved out of the way, and Juice 9mm hit the other man three times from the side, as it knocked him back, and Fifty's two shots hit him in the stomach, finishing him off. Fat Tony began shooting three shots at Juice missing him by a couple of inches, but it hit a fat white lady in the butt while she was standing at the pizza stand ordering herself a couple of slices of pizza.

"Fuck," Fat Tony said, as he jumped over the brick tile rail and grabbed the black bag with the money in it.

When he did this another one of Fat Tony's men stood up and started shooting at Fifty. Fifty scrambled to duck behind the brick tile wall trying to dodge the third man's bullets.

Just then Fifty heard three silent shots ring out from a distance and looked over and saw Baby Tank inside one of the clothing stores across the way, bustin' at a distance.

Baby Tank's three shot's hit Fat Tony's third man in the back and dropped him dead. Ra and Y.G. had everyone in the clothing store lay down on the ground.

Juice handed Summer his other 9mm and jumped up bustin' at Fat Tony again, as Fat Tony tried to run away with the money.

A bullet hit fat Tony in the back of his arm and it made him turn around bustin', then he tried running again as Fifty bust four shots at him with the Desert Eagle hitting him in the shoulder and upper arm knocking the bag loose from his hand as money flew everywhere.

Suddenly, a security guard pulled his gun on Juice and said, "Freeze", and Summer opened fired on him leaving him twisted on the floor. Just then two more security guards ran up behind Fifty shooting as one bullet caught him once in the back, then out of no-where Baby G, Trouble, and Little G-nut came out shooting and gunned down the two security guards before they knew what hit them.

Fat Tony was trying to scoop-up the money in the bag, as his other three crew members who was watching from the other side of the mall, ran over to help him get away. They started bussin back at Fifty, Baby G, Trouble and Little G-nut, but the youngsters had them out gunned as Trouble and G-nut both had Mac 10's and Baby G had a pistol grip 12 gage shot gun that cleared the crowd, as everyone was running and ducking in a panic.

Fifty ran over to Summer and Juice and gave Summer his ski mask and said, "Put this on, and let's roll."

Fifty grabbed her by the hand and they zigged-zagged through the crowd.

As they watched Baby Tank gun down two of the three men that was protecting Fat Tony, and Fat Tony grab his chrome 45 automatic out, and bust three more shots at Baby Tank that was across from the action, and went to turn and run away, and didn't see the old man that was in

the wheel chair sitting six feet from Fat Tony as the old
man was trying to cover up from getting shot, and Fat
Tony tripped over the old man's chair, and the money flew
everywhere again.

Fat Tony looked at the man in the wheel chair, and
shot him twice in the face, blowing half his head off.

Ra and Y.G. was running down the opposite side of
the mall shooting at Fat Tony and his last crew member, as
Fat Tony's last crew member pulled out his big 44
magnum and exchanged five shots back, then tried to grab
the other dead crew members 45 automatic from the dead
man's hand, and Fifty and Juice emptied the rest of their
clip all up in his body.

Fat Tony saw this and decided to try to make a run for
it as everyone opened fired.

A off duty police officer ran from no where and open
fired on Baby G, as Trouble and Little G-nut ate him up
with multiple gun shots.

Fifty ran and stopped by the money and told Summer
to grab it. She started scooping as much as she could in
the bag as Fifty saw one of the crew members reaching for
his gun while bleeding on the ground, and Fifty shot him
four times with the big 45 automatic.

"Come on let's go." Fifty yelled out loud as Juice and
Little G-nut was carrying Baby G and Trouble was behind
them watching their back as Ra, Y.G., and Baby Tank ran
up too.

"We got to get out of here! Juice, Little G-nut, Ra, and
Trouble – ya'll carry Baby G in a four man hold like a
stretcher Baby Tank and Y.G. cover the rear, and I'll lead
the way." Fifty said, as he looked at Summer and said,
"you follow me!"

"We got company," Baby Tank said as him and Y.G.
reloaded and started bustin at the police who arrived on
the scene, and was headed toward them. Everybody
started following Fifty and Summer as they headed

toward the door through J.C. Penny's. Fifty seen a police coming his way, and he let both of his 45 automatics loose on him, lifting the police man off his feet, and laid him on the ground shaking in a puddle of blood as he shook to his death.

Fat Tony was bleeding pretty bad as he made it to the parking lot, running wildly with his gun in his hand looking for away out, then a woman said, "do you need a ride Sir?" As she pulled up in a burgundy truck, and Fat Tony seen the black lady and was glad that someone would stop to help him as he ran around the passenger side of the truck, and opened up the door to jump in, and saw a 3.80 automatic looking him straight in his eyes as Tee-Tee said, "Checkmate!" And shot Fat Tony five times in the face and head, dropping him dead on the parking lot ground. "That's for my sister bitch!" She said as she drove off.

Fifty opened up the door to the parking lot, as he and Summer held the double doors open for his crew, and they carried Baby G outside of the mall into the parking structure. Little G-nut gave Baby G legs to Trouble, and said, "I'll go grab the bucket and ran off, just then a police car swooped up and two police officer's tried to jump out of the police car, but they never made it, because everyone started bustin at them filling them up with bullet holes. Fifty and Trouble was walking up on them, as they were shooting the shit out of the police, hitting them multiple times, leaving them twisted on the ground and full of lead. Fifty said, "let's take the damn police car as a burgundy Escalade pulled up, and everyone pointed their guns at the vehicle, Tee-Tee said, "get in – let's roll!"

"Oh, shit that my girl, get in ya'll!" Fifty uttered as Summer ran over and jumped into the passenger seat, and they throw Baby G into the back seat as Fifty, Ra, and Trouble jumped into the truck, and Juice looked at his comrades and said, "I can't leave yet, I got to make sure my homies make it, take Baby G to Annie Mae, she'll get him right." And Juice shut the door as Tee-Tee rolled out.

Baby Tank and Y.G. was running and shooting as they tried to hold the police off for enough time so their comrades can get away, then they tried to make it around to the outside door so they could get away too. Two police men were creeping up from behind them, when they heard five shots coming from their rear, they turned and saw two police-men laid out on the tile, and Juice was standing behind them. Juice said, "Come on ya'll let's roll B!" They followed Juice outside and Little G-nut pulled up in the G-ride bucket and they jumped in and rolled out.

A police car was coming into the parking lot when they saw little G-nut turn out into the streets, and they instantly busted a u-turn and started chasing them. "Turn here and pull over Nut, we got to get them off our trail before re-enforcement comes!" Juice said, as Little G-nut hit the corner and stopped, and they jumped out and as the police car hit the corner after them, the police saw the car stopped in the middle of the street and slammed on his brakes as Juice and the youngsters all started running up to the police car shooting. The policeman saw three mask men running up to them with fire coming out of their hands, and the police never had a chance to react, as the bullets had no mercy. Juice and the youngsters ran and jumped back into the G-ride and punched out, as the two old black men on the corner started cheering for the bad guys.

* * * *

Baby G was leaking blood pretty bad, he got hit three times, once in the chest, once in the stomach, and once in the hip, and Mrs. Anne Mae was hard at work on him. Fifty had a bullet wound in his upper back, that Tee-Tee was holding a rag on, trying to stop the bleeding. Ra had a small in and out bullet wound on his arm that Summer was attending too.

"Yo Ma, you see the type of shit that a nigga went through for you – you better not ever think about doing my man wrong, Or I'll beat you up myself!" Ra said, as everyone laughed and Summer kissed him on the cheek and said, "you know damn well I love him!" And smiled at him.

Juice, Y.G., and Little G-nut walked into the apartment and Little G-nut said, "Yo what's the word Rade!" And everyone jumped up excited and gave them a big hug.

It took Mrs. Annie Mae forty-five minutes to get the slugs out of Baby G and stop the bleeding, and with a little rest, he should make it. Mrs. Annie Mae took the bullet out of Fifty's back and he was as good as new. Ra just got sewed up and he was cool. Mrs. Annie Mae needed supplies for Baby G to nurse him back to health and some pain pills to hold him over until he heals, so Fifty dug into his black duffle bag and gave her $3,000 thousand dollars for supplies, and an extra $10,000 for her service. She tried to decline but Fifty insisted, and he gave his crew 20g's a piece, and make Y.G, Trouble, and Baby G all 'G.S.', which stand for 'Gorilla Sergeants', which gives them all the power to recruit other comrades.

The shoot out was all over the news station, and it was a million dollar reward for information to the arrest of the unknown masked murders.

Sixteen people died in the hideous shoot out, and nine more people were injured. Eight of the sixteen people who died were peace officers, so the man hunt was on. Fifty told his crew to lay low, and they all knew that it was a must that they all vow silent and secrecy, and if anyone should utter a peep of the incident to anyone, and it gets back, then they would kill him instantly. The law was made and everyone understood the consequences. Everyone embraced and Fifty and his ladies had a new found love for his comrades as they left.

* * * *

Summer took Fifty to get Nina's body from the big garbage container that Fat Tony dumped her dead body in, so that they could put her properly to rest. Tee-Tee told Fifty and Summer about how she caught Fat Tony slippin, and Fifty was captivated by the down and real ladies that he had on his team. Summer and Tee-Tee pampered Fifty for a week straight, spoiling him to death. They knew that he was down for them to the fullest, and they called each other his million dollar ladies. Fifty couldn't help but to love and appreciate them for the thorough women that they were to him, and knew that they both was priceless. Summer and Tee-Tee brung three more beautiful ladies to the stable, and it was on. They brung a beautiful chocolate sista' named CoCo that was gorgeous in the face and thick in the ass and hips with little sexy tits. She stood 5'3" and was as sexy as a woman can get. The second lady was a pretty Asian woman name Tia, who was little and petite with a pretty innocent face and nice fat butt on her. She was raised in Harlem, so she was black in spirit and could cross over like an actress! Then there was Angel, a real pretty Puerto Rican girl who was bronze complexion with a face like an angel and a body like a stripper. Fifty knew that he had the baddest bitches in the game. And they all brung in $4,000 dollars a week or better, so business was good.

Fifty took Summer and Tee-Tee out to dinner to kick it with them, and get the run down on the business and what they needed to do to improve it. Summer and Tee-Tee gave their opinion and they decided to go dancing at a popular club called the Q Club, it was packed wall to wall, as niggas and ladies got their groove on. Fifty and his two super models dance for about three songs, and was feeling good as they enjoyed each others company.

The DJ introduced a new hot cut that was about to hit the streets on 'The Hood Mix Tape,' the DJ dropped the song and Fifty's mind was in shock as his song came over the speakers." Daddy, that sounds just like you!"

"It is me baby – I did the song for a associate of mine for some promotional shit, and he got it on the air." Fifty started rappin his lyrics as Summer and Tee-Tee sat in shock never knowing that their man could rap. They always seen him write some stuff down on his note pad, but never heard him put it down before. The DJ played the song twice and Fifty was floating on cloud nine. They left the club half drunk, horny, and feeling good, and Fifty told Summer to pull over so he could go buy some Hennessy at the store. They pulled up and Fifty jumped out to go buy the drinks and condoms, and passed by a black BMW with dark tinted windows but didn't pay it no mind.

"Yo, Yo, Yo, kid! Look, ain't that that muthafucka Fifty."

"It sure in the fuck is B!"

"Yo, I'ma wet this nigga up Sun – pull over there so we can roll out quick." And the BMW pulled down the street a bit.

Fifty came out of the store with a pint of Hennessy and a 12 pack of Magnums, and had intentions on using them all. As Fifty was walking toward Summers truck a nigga step out and said, "Yo Fifty!" Fifty turned around not trippin or aware of what was going down, and his eyes got big as he saw a man with a black fitted New York baseball cap holding up a 9mm Gloc, and shot the mess out of Fifty.

Fifty fell to the parking lot pavement as the bullets took him by surprise. Summer and Tee-Tee yelled as they jumped out of the truck bustin at the man running down the street, he staggered a bit, and then jumped into the black BMW as the car burned rubber away from the curb and Summer unloaded the rest of her bullets into the back window of the car. The car turned the corner and was gone. As Summer said, "Let's get him to the truck and take him to the hospital." They carried him to the truck and put him in the back seat and Summer started driving like a preacher running from hell, as she swerved in and out of traffic. Tee-Tee called Juice and told him what happened, and they was on their way to meet them at the hospital. Summer pulled into the emergency in record timing, and she jumped out to grab a doctor as they put Fifty on a gurney and wheeled him into the surgery room.

Juice, Baby G, and Ra got there five minutes after, and calmed the ladies down, and made them go wash the gun powder residue up off their hands before the police arrived.

Two hours later, a doctor came out and told the ladies that Fifty was stable, and that he would make it. He got shot nine times but, his fate wasn't judged by the bullets, but more so, only the strength and plan of Gods will. Given new life to the Natural Born Gangster...!

THE END
September 19, 2013
"Ghettotheory Publishing"

**Coming December 2013,
The coldest West Coast tail every told.**

LOOK FOR *G. PRINCE* LATEST NEW
RELEASES IN BOOK STORES AND FOR
PURCHASE ON

www.ghettotheory.com
AMAZON.COM

FOR ADDITIONAL COPIES OF
NATURAL BORN GANGSTER GO TO:

HTTPS:WWW.CREATESPACE.COM/4423349/
INTER DISCOUNT CODE: YRADWL7U

Ghetto Theory Publishing

Presents

Ghetto Games

Ghetto Games II, "the saga continues."

Am I My Sister's Keeper?

**Rules of the Street Game that Every Hustler
Should Know...!**

Look for *"Ghetto Games III"*
coming soon March 2014

www.ingramcontent.com/pod-product-compliance
Lightning Source LLC
Chambersburg PA
CBHW070834120626
46556CB00002B/756